Holding
Up the Earth

Holding
Up the Earth

DIANNE E. GRAY

Houghton Mifflin Company
Boston

www.houghtonmifflinbooks.com

The text of this book is set in 13-point Old Style 7.

Book design by Celia Chetham

Library of Congress Cataloging-in-Publication Data

Gray, Dianne E.
Holding up the earth / by Dianne E. Gray
p.   cm.
Summary: Fourteen-year-old Hope visits her new foster mother's
Nebraska farm and, through old letters, a diary, and stories,
gets a vivid picture of the past in the voices of four girls her age
who lived there in 1869, 1900, 1936, and 1960.
HC ISBN 0-618-00703-2   PA ISBN 0-618-73747-2
[1. Farm life — Nebraska — Fiction. 2. Frontier and pioneer life
— Nebraska — Fiction. 3. Nebraska — Fiction.
4. Foster home care — Fiction. 5. Mothers and daughters — Fiction.
6. Letters — Fiction. 7. Diaries — Fiction.] I. Title.
PZ7.G7763Ho   2000
[Fic] — dc21
99-052637

Manufactured in the United States of America
QUM 10 9 8 7 6 5 4 3 2

For my daughters, Leanne and Shelley

Acknowledgments

Heartfelt thanks to: my professors in the MALS program at Hamline University, especially Mary François Rockcastle, who encouraged and inspired me to grow an idea into a book; Kirsten Dierking and Kay Korsgaard, fellow writers and enduring friends, who graciously read and commented on every draft; and Amy Flynn, the champion and editor of this book, whose keen eye and illuminating questions helped me to weed the thorny thistle from the wildflowers.

If you wish to visit this book's Web site, you will find it at: www.prairievoices.com.

This land is the house
we have always lived in.
The women,
their bones are holding up the earth.

— Linda Hogan, from
"Calling Myself Home"

Holding Up the Earth

One

"New digs." This was a thing my mother had always said when we packed our stuff and moved to a new place, which before the accident we'd done more times than I have fingers to count. But the only thing new to these digs was me. Sarah, my latest foster mom, and I had arrived at Anna's farm earlier that day. For Sarah, the move from Minnesota to Nebraska meant a homecoming. For me, the move was just another going-away.

Muffled voices rose through the heat grate in the bedroom floor: Sarah's voice, then Anna's voice, blending so rhythmically they sounded as if they were singing rounds in a mother-daughter song. I'd been down there a few minutes before, sitting with them at the kitchen table, listening as they reminisced about old times. But Sarah had kept trying to draw me into their conversation, so I'd excused myself by saying I wanted to unpack.

I shifted their voices to the background and pulled my backpack into my lap. I'd had the backpack for a long time and never went anywhere without it, never. As a result, it was pretty

1

beat-up. A large safety pin held one of the shoulder straps in place; a strip of duct tape bandaged a gash in Garfield's smile. Carrying a kid's backpack hadn't won me many friends, especially after I'd entered middle school. I didn't care. My mother had bought the backpack for me the week before I started first grade. She had tried to talk me into choosing one of the plainer, more practical ones on display at Target, but I'd said I'd just die if I didn't have the bright red one. On the way home from that shopping trip, our car was broadsided by a drunk driver. I didn't die, but my mother did.

After tugging open the stubborn zipper, I began to pull my memories from the backpack: the speckled stone I'd accidentally pitched through the window at one foster home, the front-door key from another, a joker from the deck of cards I'd learned to play solitaire with — one item from each of the seven foster homes I'd lived in. I always chose something small and portable, but something that held special meaning, like the small flashlight I'd used the night of my first dream search. Though I took these things without permission, I always left something of mine in their place — a picture I had drawn, a lopsided toothpick sculpture, one of my baby teeth.

Next out were my earth-finds: a cameo pin I'd

discovered while sifting through the dirt at a downtown Minneapolis excavation site; the glass eye I'd pried out of the mud along the Mississippi River; and the silver spoon I'd found while sorting through the rubble of an old house that was being torn down. The oldest of these earth-finds, a triangular pottery shard, dated back to the summer before my mother died. I'd dug up the shard with my plastic shovel, somewhere in New Mexico, on a trip my mother had saved two years' worth of waitressing tips to take. That had been her dream, someday to save enough money so she could go to college and become a real archaeologist.

Last out, as always, was the Ziploc bag. Inside the bag was yet another bag, and inside the inside bag was a handful of dove gray ashes. I closed my eyes and pressed the bag against my cheek, hoping this time I'd be able to remember my mother's face. This part of my nightly ritual was getting harder. I'd been six when she died, and I'd just turned fourteen. She'd been ashes for more years than she'd been my living, breathing mother.

There had been more of her in the beginning, but the urn was heavy and my hands were small. Shortly after being placed in my first foster home, I'd dropped the urn, and the ashes had poured onto the floor. I was frantically spooning my mother back into the urn when my foster mom walked into the room. After she helped me scoop most of the ashes up, she pulled me into her lap and, with a caring voice, said it was time I chose a place for my mother to rest. The next day my foster mom drove me around for what seemed like hours, until I spotted an open space near a small creek. In the space grew clumps of tall white flowers, snowflake shaped, which my foster mom said were Queen Anne's lace. And there were butterflies, monarchs, dozens of them, their flight like a ballet as I tearfully released all but a baggie full of ashes into the air. Though I dreamed of that field, searched for it whenever I could, in daylight and in dark, I never found it again.

There were other things in my backpack, everyday things like a comb and lip gloss, things I took out only when I needed them. And there was one thing, buried at the bottom, which I hadn't taken out in years — a copy of my birth certificate, with its glaring blank space where the name of my father should have been.

I had just stuffed the last of my memories into the backpack when I heard footsteps on the stairs, then footsteps coming down the hall.

"Hope, may I come in?" Sarah asked.

"It's your room," I answered.

Sarah stepped in. "Not anymore. This is your room now. And we must do some redecorating. This place is like a museum of the sixties."

"It's you," I said, forcing a smile.

"In another life."

Sarah moved about the room, stopping for a moment in front of each of the posters that dotted the walls. One read, "Make Love, Not War." On another, a brilliant white peace symbol leaped out of a black background. And there was one of the Beatles smiling from under nerdy hair.

"The next time we drive into Prairie Hill, you'll have to choose some posters of your own."

"I like the room the way it is," I said.

Sarah turned to me and smiled. "Are you sure?"

I nodded.

I did like the room the way it was, but not because of the posters or the pink-and-white quilt that was spread over the bed. I liked the room because it was a place where memories didn't have to be hidden to be safe. Besides, if things didn't work out, I wasn't big on the idea of leaving too much of myself behind.

"Mom and I are planning to get an early start in the meadow, and we were hoping you'd join us. It's especially beautiful there this time of year."

"I'll think about it," I said. In the nine months I'd lived with Sarah I'd learned that saying "I'll think about it" was a better answer than "no." Words like *no* or phrases like *I can't* were broken things to Sarah — broken things she'd just have to fix.

When Sarah had finished rearranging her high school debate trophies and brushed nonexistent dust from the picture of her father, she sat next to me on the bed and bounced a couple of times. "I should buy you a new mattress. This one's as soft as a marshmallow."

"It's fine, better than most."

"And this?" she said, plumping the pillow. "I'll bet you'd prefer foam over feathers."

"The pillow's fine, too."

Sarah smoothed a wrinkle in the quilt.

"Did you make the quilt?" I asked before Sarah had a chance to suggest a different one.

"I did, with lots of help from my grandmother. She had patient hands."

Just then Anna poked her head around the half-open door. "Is this a private party?" she asked.

"A private party for three," Sarah answered.

I'd met Anna once before, when she'd driven her old Ford pickup truck to Minneapolis to spend Christmas with us. Anna was easy. Being with her was like taking a test where every answer is the right one.

Anna's face mirrored Sarah's, though Anna's was etched with deeper age lines. Both women were tall and walked in the same purposeful way. The only real physical difference between them was the size of their breasts. Anna's were large, and Sarah's, like mine, were not.

"Thought I should warn you that my house is in the habit of complaining about her creaky joints in the night," Anna said.

"No problem. I don't do the worry thing," I said as a way of stopping the sudden memory flood of first nights in strange houses, each with its own set of creepy hum-clunk-whir-clank noises.

"Good, then you won't mind my ghosts, either," Anna said, grinning.

"Mom's teasing," Sarah said, then yawned. "But I'll feel like a ghost tomorrow if I don't get to bed. It's been a very long day."

I admired Sarah's ability to shift from fast-forward to sleep in a matter of minutes. Sleep for me would be hours away.

"If you need anything, I'll be just down the hall," Sarah said, moving toward the door. "Sleep well."

"Sleep well," Anna echoed.

I listened as Sarah and Anna said their good nights in the hallway, and then, reaching for my backpack, my hand brushed over the spot where Sarah had been sitting. The quilt was still warm. I held my hand there until the hallway grew quiet.

After that, I finally unpacked. The large suitcase, which held all the clothes Sarah had bought for me, I shoved under the bed. The smaller suitcase, I balanced across the arms of the rocking chair, then unzipped and opened the lid. Inside, besides the few clothes I liked to wear, lay my sketchpads. I fanned these out across the bed. The oldest ones weren't real sketchpads, just school tablets and spiral-bound notebooks, whatever I'd been able to get my hands on.

Thumbing through my drawings was like watching myself grow up. In the earliest ones, my people resembled tadpoles. Twig arms and legs stuck out of their heads. With time, my figures took on a more natural shape: arms and legs grew out of oval torsos, lashes curled up from almond-shaped eyes, and fingers appeared at the ends of hands.

A middle school art class had marked a dramatic change. Mr. Montgomery, the teacher, had taught me to use shape and shading to bring my drawings to life. He'd also said I was bursting with raw talent. I'd been suspicious at first, having learned that expected favors sometimes followed praise. But when Mr. Montgomery continued treating me, and everyone else in our class, in a warm, respectful way, I'd let myself believe he might be telling the truth and worked even harder on my drawing. This pleased Mr. Montgomery so much he offered to lend me books on drawing technique, which pleased me so much I'd slip a note inside the books before I returned them.

The first notes simply read, "Thanks a lot, Hope," but as time went on, I wrote longer notes, telling him what a terrific teacher he was or how lucky his children were to have a dad like him, things like that. On the last day of school, before returning the last book, I wrote my last note on the back of a foster care application form, then waited half the summer for him to call. The other half of the summer I spent making sure that come fall I'd be in another foster home, another school. I did this by refusing to eat.

I balanced a sketchpad over my crossed legs and penciled images I remembered from that day's nine-hour road trip — a highway, wide at its base and arching from left to right, narrowing to a point before dissolving over the horizon, and by the side of this road, as if patiently waiting, a small child's tennis shoe. Tree branches poked through the roof of an abandoned farmhouse. On the porch of this house, I added a rocking chair, then I licked my finger and smudged it, creating the eerie rocking motion I'd observed through the window of the car. Cornstalks sprouted from the leftover spaces. Pleased with this collage of images, I signed a practiced and flamboyant "Hope" in the lower right-hand corner.

I then flipped to a fresh page, where I meant to draw images of the town of Prairie Hill, where Sarah had given me "the tour" before stocking up on groceries at the Bag-N-Save. But the places Sarah had shown me weren't places I could see. "Over there," she'd said, "that's where the old courthouse used to stand. And there, across the street, that boarded-up building was once the movie theater." It was the same on every block. A thing that had been there when Sarah was a girl, a place that she had loved, wasn't there anymore. I finally settled on a single image — a shopping cart that was rolling away, escaping maybe, from the crowded parking lot of Wal-Mart.

Then, after tucking my hair behind my ears and steadying myself with a deep breath, I sketched my mother's face. My hand moved slowly, deliberately, and when I had finished, I studied what I had drawn. There was something familiar in the eyes, but the mouth was wrong, the curve of the cheek, the hair. I slammed the sketchpad to the floor, then hugged my knees to my chest. I sat that way for a long time, rocking back and forth, angry with myself for allowing Sarah to bring me so far away from the places my mother and I had once shared.

Sarah hadn't told me about her plans for the summer until she'd had everything worked out. I'd panicked and called Ms. Korsgaard, my current caseworker, begging her to find me another foster home, quick. She'd said there were none available and that even if there were, she wouldn't consider them because she'd already given Sarah permission to take me out of state, and that Sarah was the best foster mom I'd ever had or could hope to have.

Though I wasn't happy with Ms. Korsgaard's answer, I couldn't argue with what she'd said. Sarah was *different* from any of my other foster moms. Her last name was Foster, which made her my Foster foster mom. She'd never been a mom before — not to other foster kids, not to kids of her own. When she'd first taken me in, she had laughingly said I'd have to teach her how. And she was *better,* because she didn't demand gratitude, as many of the others had. If I had shrunk a quarter-inch each time a foster mom told me I should be grateful she'd taken me in, I'd have disappeared completely by the age of ten. Sarah was also the only foster parent who had deposited her monthly foster care checks into a college fund account with my name on it. Last, Sarah had said I could stay with her for as long as I wanted, that she wasn't planning to take in any other foster kids. What I wanted was for the next four years to pass as quickly as possible. What I wanted was to "age out" of the foster care system. What I wanted was to be totally on my own, free, the way my mother had been.

That's why being placed with Sarah had been such a relief. With her there were no foster brothers' roving hands, no foster sisters spreading lies about me at school, no foster parents changing their minds about adopting me when they found out they were going to have a baby of their own, no foster mom snooping in my backpack and thinking my mother's ashes were a new kind of drug. I'd told Sarah at our first meeting that I was no longer interested in adoption. She'd said she'd never force me to do anything I didn't freely choose to do, so staying with her for the next four years seemed doable.

Not that Sarah was easy. She'd been the most in-your-face foster mom I'd ever had. No drawing until my homework was done, no R-rated movies from the video store, no Mountain Dew before noon, and no sleeping in, not even on weekends. Weekends were, as Sarah put it, "for giving some-thing back."

She taught peace studies at the university dur-ing the week and volunteered on the weekends. In the nine months I'd lived with Sarah, I'd ladled soup at a homeless shelter, blistered my feet on a walkathon for breast cancer research, lugged sandbags before a flood, and shoveled mud out of basements after. I'd read stories to kids in a women's shelter and stuffed a zillion envelopes. I didn't mind. Sarah kept us so busy we didn't have to think up things to say to each other when we were alone in her apartment. But on the trip from Minnesota to Nebraska, we'd had nothing but time, and Sarah had hinted at adoption, saying, "If you like it in Nebraska, I could find a teaching job there, and we could make it permanent."

But I'd promised myself I wouldn't sign my

name to Sarah's happy ending, even if it meant I'd have to bug Ms. Korsgaard until she found me a new foster home when we returned to Minneapolis in the fall.

I pulled the beaded chain on the lamp that sat on the bedside table, lay back on the bed, and worked at emptying my mind, a trick that sometimes helped me fall asleep. But that night the emptiness never happened. The quiet was too loud. Sarah had said this quiet was one of the things she liked best about living in the country. But lying there that night, surrounded by silence, only made me imagine what it must be like to be dead. So I filled the void with my listening: the steady in and out of my breath, the tick, tick, tick of the wind-up clock, the mousy rustling in the wall. From the air outside the open window, I gathered in cricket chirps, the distant hoot of an owl. I listened until I crowded the silence out.

Eventually I did fall asleep, but only long enough to relive "the dream." It was night. I stood in a field of tall grass and flowers. The moon was full, but it only shone in a circle at my feet. From somewhere in the blackness beyond, my mother called to me. "Where will I find you?" I asked, running in the direction of her voice. The circle of light ran with me, ran with me even when I tried to outsmart it and leap to the side, ran with me into that foggy place between awake and asleep. I grabbed my backpack and slipped out of bed. Thinking I was back in Sarah's first-floor apartment, I unhooked the window screen and eased myself out. Instead of dropping to the ground, my bare feet hit something scratchy and solid, almost immediately. I felt around with my big toe. Shingles, on the slant. Fully awake by then, I remembered where I was.

"If you're looking for the rose trellis, it's a bit to the right."

My head jerked to the left. There, framed in a square of window light, sat Anna, her feet dangling over the edge of the porch roof, her white hair let down from its daytime bun.

"I . . . I . . . needed some fresh air," I said, trying to hide my backpack.

"In that case, why don't you scoot over and join me."

I scooted carefully, glad that I hadn't bothered to change out of my clothes.

"Have you ever seen such a gorgeous sky?" she asked.

I looked up. Above me the sky was studded with more stars than I had ever seen. "Cool," I said.

"Cool," Anna repeated, imitating the way I'd said this word.

"Way cool," I added.

"Nifty way cool," Anna said. At this we both laughed, a thing I wasn't in the habit of doing.

"When I was a girl and said words like *nifty* and *swell,* I spent a lot of time out here, waiting for one of those stars to fall so I could make a wish."

"You lived here when you were a girl?"

"Born right in there, in Mama's cherrywood bed."

Envy bubbled up inside me. "It must be nice, to live inside your memories."

Anna broke her eyes away from the stars and turned them on me. "I never really thought of it quite like that, living inside my memories. But I suppose you're right. Most of the important things that happened in my life happened on this farm. Isn't one dish in my cupboards, one box up in the attic, one plowed field that doesn't have a story connected to it, that doesn't have a history."

"How far back do the memories go?"

"Well, I suppose they go all the way back to Abigail, whose father homesteaded this land in 1869."

I pulled my backpack into my lap and ran my fingers over its fabric.

Anna touched my arm. "Perhaps you'd be interested in reading Abigail's letters. She was about your age when she wrote them."

I knew what Anna was up to. Memories weren't like the sky; they couldn't be shared. "I'll think about it," I said.

"Why don't we climb back inside, and I'll give the letters to you; then they'll be handy."

Anna crawled to the window, then stopped and looked back. "Maybe you should go in first. That way you can help me through."

I crawled, the pebbles from the shingles digging into my knees. At the window, I pulled the screen away at the bottom, ducked my head under, then sat down on the sill and swung my legs inside.

"Oh, to be young again," Anna said, her grip on my outstretched hand stronger than I had expected.

At her dresser, she opened the lid on an ornately carved wooden box, withdrew a bundle of yellowing letters, handed them to me, and then said, "Goodness, look at the time. We'd both better try to get some sleep. Sarah has plans for us tomorrow."

"Big plans," I said as I headed for the door.

"Cool plans," Anna said as I entered the hall.

I tiptoed past the room Sarah was sleeping in, though this probably wasn't necessary. Sarah slept as intensely as she lived. Without turning on the light in her old room, I dropped the letters on the nightstand and lay down on the bed. Hugging my backpack to my chest, I filled the black air with imaginary stars, held them there, then let them fall one at a time.

A glittery comet was streaking across my imaginary sky when an odor I hadn't noticed before distracted me. I sniffed the air, my backpack, and the border of the quilt. When I pulled the lamp chain, light spilled over the letters. I lifted them to my nose — old wood, a faint scent of rose, and something else. Time maybe. "Okay, I'll read," I whispered.

Two

May 3, 1869

My dearest cousin Rachel,

I pray this letter finds you well. Perhaps I should say, "I pray this letter finds its way to you." Father has brought Mother and me to the middle of nowhere. The nearest town where I might post letters is a half day's ride to the north, though it requires a far stretch of the imagination to call Prairie Hill a town. Not like back home in Ohio. There are but a few wooden shanties and Fowler's General Store. Father says now that Nebraska is open to settlers the town will soon grow into a bustling city. I have my doubts, but I humor him with agreement. You know Father, always the optimist.

Fetch Uncle John's atlas, and I will help you pinpoint the location of Father's homestead. Have you returned? Good. Turn to the page which maps out the territory west of the

Missouri River, the region labeled "The Great American Desert." Rotate the map a quarter turn clockwise, so west is at the top, and trace your eyes along the course of the Platte River, beginning at the point where it converges with the Missouri. Now ponder the shape the river forms. Do you see her? The profile of a young woman's face? I pray your eyes see what mine have seen on Father's map, else you will surely think me daft. Now imagine that the river does not rise at an angle from her brow, but arcs gently to form the crown of her head. If you imagine in the proper proportions, the point where you are so fond of pinning your satin bows marks the place on the map where I am to be found. See me there, that tiny speck, smiling and waving up at you?

Now that you know my whereabouts, I will tell you of the final leg of our journey west. Shortly after posting my last letter to you, on the levee at Nebraska City, Father hurried straightaway to the land office. After hitching the team to the rail, he removed his cap, combed his fingers through his hair, and climbed the steps with such haste you would have thought they were giving away pints of ale instead of land. Mother and I, proper women that we are, waited on the seat of the wagon. Mother waited patiently. I squirmed and fidgeted until Mother bade me be still. At this, I pushed my impatience deep inside, where it danced a private jig. When Father finally burst from the door, he let out a raucous holler and tossed his cap high into the air. He had filed a homestead claim on prime land, 160 acres in Prairie County, for the mere cost of ten dollars and a promise to live on the land for the next five years.

Father took up the reins and said, "Let's go home." *Yes,* I thought, *let's go home.* These words were like a salve for my travel-weary spirit.

We followed the Nebraska City Cut-Off, part of the old Oregon Trail, and four days later we arrived in Prairie Hill. The date was April the seventeenth. A portent of good fortune, don't you think? Arriving at our destination on my fourteenth birthday.

While Father bargained over the price of a plow with Mr. J. Fowler, the young, ruddy-faced proprietor of the general store, Mother and I inspected the wares. Lined up along the raw wood shelves was a smattering of the usual staples — flour and sugar and coffee, salt and tobacco, hardtack biscuits and nails — but a fearful lack of purely womanly interests. Mother, quite out of character, sashayed up to the dusty counter and boldly asked,

"And where, my good man, shall I find the yard goods?" Mr. J. Fowler spat a stream of tobacco at a hitherto unwashed and foul-smelling spittoon. "Hasn't been a need, ma'am. Aren't any women in these parts, save for old Lulu Piper. Most men come on ahead, to prove up their land before sending for their womenfolk." The color drained from Mother's cheeks and, if I had had a mirror, I imagine from my cheeks as well. At least until Mr. J. Fowler winked at me, which caused my cheeks to fill again, with coal-fire heat. I was glad Mother had turned away and did not witness this indelicate act.

Mother said not a word as we left the last hint of civilization behind and headed out onto the open prairie. She sat statue still, save for her hands, which were busy wringing one another. Though I tried to remain loyal to Mother, to mask my excitement, Father's exuberant chatter nibbled at my resolve until I was quite giddy with anticipation. "There, to the left," he said, "all the homesteading men will build a school. And there, to the right, a church. A church with a fine steeple bell. Can you hear it, Abby girl? Can you hear the bell ringing?" Oh, Rachel, I did hear that bell, a whole carillon of bells, pealing out across the empty prairie.

Near sunset, we arrived at the banks of Beaver Creek. After six long weeks, for better or worse, we had come home.

Mother and I have set up housekeeping a short distance north of the creek. Our roof is fashioned from sky and our floor from a carpet of laid-over prairie grass. The table, upon which I now write, occupies the center of this space. Mother and Father make their bed in the wagon. On rainy nights I must join them, but when the sky is dry, I choose to sleep on a bedroll laid out under the stars. I imagine you staring into the same sky, wishing on the same stars. It helps me not to miss you so much.

Father has begun to plow open a field. His work begins at dawn and does not cease until the last glimmer of twilight. Plowing is backbreaking work. How do I know it is backbreaking work? you ask. I know it to be true because I have done it myself. Yes. For brief periods of time each day, to give Father a needed rest, I guide the plow through the thick sod. What a sense of power, to command the brutish oxen with a "Gee" and a "Haw" and a "Whoa," to feel their movement through the heavy leather reins.

There is a certain pleasure in this work — watching the fresh-turned soil curl off the blade, smelling the earthy aroma, tasting the salt from the beads of perspiration that gather on my brow. And how satisfying it is to look back over the furrow I have plowed and think, *This is the work I have done, the progress I have made.* So different it is from women's work, which, as you well know, seems never to be done. Food is prepared, then quickly eaten. Clothing is washed, only to be soiled after but a few wearings. But sod broken once is sod broken forever.

Though I fight against it, oftentimes I measure this place by what is absent, most notably people and trees. We have not seen another living soul since arriving at our homestead, so at times it seems as if we are the only three people in the world: Adam and Eve and Abigail. Fear not that I will eat the forbidden fruit. There is little chance of that, with nary a fruit tree about. Oh, how I miss the trees: the pines, the oaks, the maples, the elms. Save for the stand of cottonwoods and one lonely willow that line the banks of the creek, the prairie stretches unbroken to the horizon. The grasses sway and swirl in the wind, and sometimes I grow faint in the watching of this waltzlike dance. There is a quiet near dusk, after the birds have settled and before the coyote has begun its howl, a silence so deep that I can almost hear the whir of thoughts spinning in my head.

I will dip the nib of my pen into the

inkwell a few more times and put an end to these ramblings by telling you of my favorite place — the meadow. It occupies some twenty acres in the southeast corner of our land, cut off from the rest by the creek. To get there I must wade its waters. This requires that I lift my petticoats up about my waist. Now you must truly think me shameless. But you would need to witness the meadow with your own eyes to understand. The creek makes a lazy loop in that spot, so the open space of the meadow is surrounded on three sides by trees. Father says someday he will use the meadow to pasture the herd of cattle he hopes to acquire. But for now it is mine. Oh, Rachel, I wish you were here to share it with me. There is a peace in the meadow, a peace like nothing I have ever experienced before. The wind, which roars fiercely and unremittingly across the open prairie, is gentled to a whisper inside the embrace of the cottonwoods. Birds make their homes in the boughs of the trees and quite fill the meadow with their songs. Each time I go for a ramble there, I feel as if I am cleansed of my loneliness and, yes, to be honest, sometimes my despair.

Write soon and tell me of everything back home. Tell me of Priscilla and Margaret and the orchard in bloom. Tell me of school and church and band concerts in Mill Run Park. Tell me of the sounds of train whistles and the clippety-clop of hoofs on cobblestone. Tell me your secrets and your dreams. Most especially tell me of Peter. Give my love to Aunt Harriet and Uncle John.

Love and prayers,
Abigail

June 12, 1869

Dearest Rachel,

Father returned from Prairie Hill with a wagonload of lumber, and in his satchel was your letter. I have read your words so many times I can recite them from memory. I felt as if I were there with you at the Methodist Church social, sitting on the quilt beside you and Peter, the taste of mincemeat pie rolling about on my tongue. And I am yet chuckling over your story of how the bumblebee entangled itself in Priscilla's hair. What a sight, her shrieking and dashing about helter-skelter. Poor thing. She must have been mortified.

Before I tell you our goings on, I will answer your questions. No, we have seen no wild Indians, at least not yet. J. Fowler has told Father that we should be on our guard because there are Pawnee about. They live on their Loop River reservation, which is two days ride north of here, but when their corn has been planted, they venture south to hunt the buffalo. And I have proof that what he said is true. Arrowheads are so numerous one would think they grew from seeds planted in the ground.

One day, when I was strolling through my meadow, I found a beaded pouch. Though the leather is hard, the beadwork is perfectly sewn. Red spirals radiate from a central yellow circle. I loosened the leather thong that laced about the top and shook the contents out. A rainbow of polished stones poured into my hand. I like to imagine that the pouch belonged to a Pawnee girl, a girl about my age. She loved the meadow as much as I. It was her place to think, her place to dream. A handsome young brave rode into the meadow one summer's afternoon and swept her away on his painted pony. The pouch fell to the ground, abandoned in her ecstasy.

Yes, I am saddened by the fact that there is no school. But there is much to be learned here: how to read the sky for signs of a storm; how to prepare a meal without eggs, butter, or milk; and how to write a letter while the pesky wind teases the pages.

And, yes, it is troublesome to know that it will be some time before I again worship in a house of God. Until such time, I will find my sermons in the wildflowers and grasses and sky.

No, there have been no new arrivals of homesteading families, so I have yet to make a new friend. Having no girlfriends is the hardest part of this place. As for boys, it makes little difference. I am yet saving myself for Peter.

Now for the news from the prairie. After Father finished clearing and planting his field of sod corn, he commenced building our house. Before I describe it you should prepare yourself for a good chuckle. Ready? It is built from blocks of prairie sod. Mother would faint dead away if she knew I was telling you this. If Aunt Harriet inquires, tell her we have a house built from marble. That's what J. Fowler calls it — prairie marble.

We went visiting, to the Piper homestead, so Father could learn how it was done. The Pipers are our nearest neighbors, if you can stretch your imagination to consider five miles as near! The Pipers are old hands at pioneering. They first broke sod on a homestead in eastern Kansas. Quite contented they were, until their neighbors learned that the Piper homestead was a stop on the Underground Railroad, that they were helping smuggle slaves to freedom in Nebraska Territory. For fear that they would be jailed or hanged, the Pipers pulled up roots and planted them here in Nebraska soil, where, thankfully, one man has never been allowed to own another.

I found out the hard way that Mrs. Lulu Piper has a keen sense of humor. I was entertaining myself by reading the walls. Yes, you heard me — reading the walls. The walls of the Piper soddy are papered over with newsprint — old editions of the *Chicago Tribune* mostly. I had read my way into the northwest corner, following a story about Indian uprisings in the Dakotas, when something tickled my leg. I shrieked when I lifted my skirts and saw that a snake had slithered up my shin. Lulu let out a hearty laugh, then picked that snake up with her bare hands and proceeded to let it coil itself about her neck. Lulu went on to tell us that it was a bull snake, harmless, really, and that she allows it to roam freely — it keeps down the population of mice who inhabit the walls. "Going to find their way in, might as well make friends." Mother's eyes were as large as Dresden saucers.

We learned from T. Piper that the best sod is to be found in buffalo wallows. They are places where the buffaloes roll, wallow, to rid themselves of long winter hair and to relieve their itching backs. These old depressions hold water during wet weather and produce a luxuriant growth of bluestem grass, whose matted roots weave a dense soil. We found such a wallow on our land. Using T. Piper's sod cutter, an odd-looking, sledlike device, Father cut a full acre of sod into rectangular blocks — eighteen inches wide, three feet long, and six inches thick. Though each block weighed upwards of fifty pounds, I helped him stack the pieces one upon the other to form the walls, leaving one space for the door, another for an isinglass window. He fashioned the roof from boards, then shingled it with sod. The price? A scant $13.75.

The roof is a bane to Mother. When it rains, water cascades down and transforms the floor into rivulets of mud. When it is dry, all manner of things fall from between the cracks in the boards. Once, when we were sitting down to supper, a dung beetle plopped into Mother's bowl of prairie chicken stew. She threw up her arms and marched outside. Father winked at me, and it was all I could do to stifle a giggle.

There is only one room in our soddy, but

with Mother's ingenuity it has taken on a homey feel. The three-hole Topsy stove stands in the northwest corner and is flanked on either side by cupboards. Mother fashioned these cupboards from wood packing crates, which she stacked end on end. Their contents are hidden from view by lengths of muslin. On the deep-set windowsill, Mother has placed her geraniums and lovingly cajoled them into full bloom. Her Seth Thomas clock chimes from its honored position on the damask-frocked steamer trunk. Father's musket hangs protectively above the door.

Housecleaning is simple. Each morning Mother gives the dirt floor a vigorous sweeping, then sprinkles it with water. Ours is yet a bit dusty, but Lulu assured us that in a short while it will become wood-plank hard. As always, Mother is fastidious. She works her straw broom into every nook and cranny because, as she says, she doesn't want any grass growing under the beds.

Mother and I planted a garden in the patch of ground where Father harvested the sod. If we can keep the rabbits and ground squirrels at bay, we should have a fine crop of potatoes, turnips, beans, onions, and melons. It was in the garden that I encountered my second snake. This time it was not a bull snake. I heard the rattle and looked up. The vile creature, its forked tongue darting out of its triangular head, was coiled not three paces away. Though my mind was awash with fright, I raised the hoe over my head and brought it down with a swift blow. I did it, Rachel, I killed the rattler before it could get me. The hoe has become my trusty companion.

To the north and west of the house we've planted rows of scrawny, slow-growing cedar saplings. These trees have a story. A Mr. Watts, who was homesteading a piece of land to the north of Prairie Hill, had ordered the trees from J. Fowler's store. Seems Mr. Watts's wife would not consent to leaving the forests of Wisconsin until he promised to plant one hundred and one trees. Can you imagine a woman being so willful? Anyway, three days after the saplings arrived by freight wagon from Omaha, and fearing they would die before being planted in the ground, J. Fowler rode out to the Watts homestead. He found Mr. Watts slumped over his plow, stone-cold dead. So, rather than have the trees suffer the same fate, J. Fowler made us a gift of them. Now that they are safely rooted in Nebraska soil, it is my task to keep them alive. Each day I tote countless buckets of water up from the creek. My arms, unused to such toil, have been praying for rain.

I like to think that the trees are our statement to this wild land that we intend to stay. Father says, "He who plants a tree loves others besides himself." The cedars will give pleasure, not only to us, but to generations who will come after us.

Now that summer has arrived, the meadow teems with life. Pink prairie roses, blue and yellow violets, wild plum blossoms, and white indigos. Quail, martins, and my favorite bird — the western meadowlark. It sings a magnificent song.

In the white glare of the midday sun, the heat becomes visible. It rises in ripples from the meadow grass. On days when the heat is especially intense, I disrobe, right down to my birthday suit, and swim in the creek. A scandalous thing, I know. But you must try it sometime. To swim with the fishes in their watery world, fingers of cool water caressing the flesh, excites a bodily pleasure I have never before imagined.

You would not recognize me now. The sun has bleached my hair the color of buttercups. My skin is bronzed, and freckles dot my face and arms. Mother fusses about my not wearing a bonnet. But it is too confining. Hinders my vision. Muffles sound. The soles of my feet are as tough as shoe leather. Yes, I have taken to going barefoot. There is a certain freedom in this — if you are vigilant, that is, and learn the art of sidestepping oxen dung, sharp rocks, and prickly cockleburs. At first Mother fretted over my indiscretion, but she did not protest too loudly. I think she may be wishing she could do the same. If I walked into the old school today, the girls would double over with laughter. But out here on the prairie I can be any way I want. There is no one to peek over the garden fence, no one to gossip over my behavior. Though I risk sounding vain, I rather like the new me.

By the time this letter reaches you, you will have celebrated your fifteenth birthday. I will be with you in spirit. You are never far from my thoughts.

With love,
Abby

P.S. Has Peter asked after me?

July 4, 1869

Rachel,

Independence Day! I can almost hear the drum and bugle corps as they parade down

Main Street, taste the fried chicken at the Odd Fellow picnic, see the fireworks exploding in the star-filled sky. Remember last year on the Fourth, when we rowed Uncle John's old skiff out on Wilson's pond? And how Peter capsized the boat trying to land that bass? How our water-soaked georgette blouses clung to our flesh? How we swam to shore and hid in rushes until Peter and William promised to cover their eyes? And how we ran all the way home, dashing in and out of bushes so we wouldn't be seen? Such fun!

Speaking of water, I've been helping Father dig a well. Since we arrived here, we have been catching rainwater in a barrel and fetching water from the creek. But we've had no rain these last few weeks, and the creek is little more than a muddy trickle. Where to dig the well was the quandary. Father studied a *Scientific American* article called "Water Witching" and decided to give it a try. He cut a branch from the willow and stripped away its leaves. Forked ends grasped in his upturned palms, he pointed the straight end out in front of him and commenced walking to and fro. The notion is this: when the willow tip passes over a place where water runs near the surface, the branch will twist in your hands and draw itself toward the ground.

After hours and hours of pacing, nothing whatsoever happened. When Father's patience wore thin, I offered to try my hand. I hadn't walked more than a few rods when the willow branch came alive in my hands. Father teases that when other settlers come he will hire me out as a "witcher."

He is digging the well by hand, and it is a frightfully slow process. He built a wooden windlass, from which he suspended a pulley and rope. One end of the rope is knotted to the oxen harness, the other to a bucket. Father sits on the bucket, and I lead the ox forward until the rope goes slack, which means Father has reached the bottom of the hole. He climbs off and starts digging. When he has filled the bucket with dirt, he gives me a holler. I lead the ox backward and up comes the bucket. I dump the dirt into an ever-enlarging pile, and the work begins anew. Father, who now refers to himself as "the world's largest prairie dog," has dug down nearly thirty feet and teases that soon he will be able to bring me back a length of silk, straight from China.

The sod corn slaps at my knees, like the saying "knee-high by the 4th of July." Father would rather have it be up to his knees, but he is content. If the harvest is as splendid as he hopes, he will purchase some chickens, a milk cow, and a sow. And if he can clear and plant more land next spring, he will build Mother a house, a real house, like the one we left back in Springfield. Personally, I don't mind the soddy. It blends into the landscape, does not blemish it with man-made clutter. The garden is up, and the ground squirrels are enjoying a heavenly feast.

Mother is "in the family way." She hasn't told me this, but I recognize the symptoms, which are not unlike the symptoms you and I secretly observed last year before the sudden appearance of Peter's baby sister. Mother's face alternates between flush red and ghostly white, the white predominating after one of her frequent forays to the privy. There is beginning to be a telltale curve to her abdomen. I wish she would take me into her confidence (now that I've become a woman myself). Questions tumble about in my head, and without you here my questions go unanswered.

Love,
Abby

P.S. Give my love to Peter.

Dear Rachel,

I am frightfully sorry for my tardiness in answering your last letter. I hope you will find it in your heart to forgive me. So much has happened I hardly know where to begin. I had best begin with the unpleasant news. The crop is gone. Yes, all of it. One night in late August, as we were about to retire for the night, a whiff of smoke curled past my nose. Afraid that a cinder from the chimney had set the roof ablaze, I rushed outside. The sky to the west glowed red. It was as if the devil himself had risen out of the bowels of the earth, bent on consuming everything in his path. Flames licked their way across the prairie like the tongues of a thousand yellow serpents. It was horrid. We wet burlap sacks at the well, then ran to the edge of the field and tried to beat out the flames. It was a losing battle from the beginning. But we had to try. Sparks skittered through the smoke-filled air and, without my knowing it, set my nightclothes on fire. Father threw me to the ground, smothering the flames with his body. Mother applied a goose-grease poultice to my burns, and the scars are healing nicely.

Fortunately the soddy was spared. Forewarned by T. Piper, Father had plowed a wide circle, a firebreak, around the house, garden, and lean-to barn. We have this, and our lives, to be grateful for.

Father drew into himself, and for three days he uttered not one word. When finally he broke his silence, he announced that he was going away to look for work — the railroad, perhaps, which is rumored to be branching out in the eastern portions of the state. His words filled me with dread. I wondered how Mother and I would manage all alone. At the same, time his words gave me hope. If he has found work, then there will be money for seed. We can start anew in spring. He's been gone four weeks now.

The Pipers left last week. When they stopped in to say their good-byes, they gave us a hindquarter of buffalo meat and made Mother a gift of their milk cow. Lulu winked at Mother, then said we had more need of the cow than they. Seems hailstones, the size of a man's fist, destroyed last year's crop, and now with the fire the Pipers are moving on and will try their luck mining for gold in Colorado. They painted a slogan on the canvas of their wagon: "In God we trusted, in Nebraska we busted." Mother took to her bed after they left.

The good news is that Mother has gotten over her funk about the Pipers' departure, and the two of us are managing quite nicely. We are preparing for winter. Using Father's pitchfork, we dug up the potatoes and stored them in burlap sacks. We jerked, smoked, and salted the buffalo meat. From the fat we rendered lard and made dipped candles. We gathered chokecherries along the creek, putting up ten pints of preserves.

I've even chopped and stacked two cords of firewood. I'm no Paul Bunyan. I don't fell any standing trees. I'm clearing out the deadwood that has fallen along the creek. As a hedge against hard times, Mother and I ventured far and wide on the prairie and gathered up buffalo chips. Lulu had told us they make a fine, warm fire.

With a bit of help from Mother, I can hitch up the team in no time at all. Tomorrow I will drive the wagon into Prairie Hill to post this letter and see if there is any word from Father. Because, as Mother likes to say, "money is as scarce as hens' teeth," I will have to ask for credit at J. Fowler's store to buy a few staples — flour, sugar, and the like.

I have saved the best news for last. Mother has taken me into her confidence. Soon after Father's departure, Mother asked if she could join me on my daily ramble in the meadow. It was quite a sight. Mother perched on the creek bank, unbuttoning her shoes and rolling off her stockings. I could hardly believe my eyes when, before wading into the stream, she lifted her skirts about her waist.

In the meadow, which nature has painted with hues of gold and copper, we spread Mother's crazy quilt over the grass and shared an intimate tête-à-tête. She told me of the baby and of the three babies who came soon after me, all born too soon. She told me that when she was my age she had dreamed of traveling to exotic places. She laughed when I asked her if she thought the prairie was exotic. I told her how Peter kissed me full on the lips before we left Springfield, and she didn't swoon. Mother is a real person — like you and me. Fancy this: she says she yet feels like a girl inside. After our chat, we lay silent for a time, watching great *V*s of wild geese honk their way through the crisp autumn sky.

I am to be her midwife. The idea of it sends a shiver through my bones, but at the same time it makes me feel responsible and womanly. It is to be a Christmas baby. If Father has had any luck finding work, it should be a time of real celebration.

All for now. Write soon,
Abby

P.S. Tell Peter to write. Mother has given permission for this scandalous breach of etiquette.

Rachel,

I don't know when I will have a chance to ride into Prairie Hill to post this letter, what with all the snow. I will begin it now and add to it as the days pass. I fear we are in the throes of a blizzard. Yesterday dawned warm and bright — too warm for this late in November. Mother, sensing a change in her joints, called the day a "weather brewer." She was right. By late afternoon the wind had shifted around to the north, and by sunset the temperature had plummeted thirty degrees. Tumbleweeds paraded like retreating Confederate soldiers across the prairie. When I went out to milk Bessie (that's what I named the Pipers' milk cow), snow was falling in big wet flakes. All night the wind howled like a wild beast. As I lay beneath my quilts, I was glad for the toasty warmth of the soddy. Its thick, earthen walls deny entrance to the icy wind.

When I arose this morning, I rubbed a

peephole in the frost-covered window. My eyes were greeted with a blinding whiteness. If I'd had my druthers, I would have snuggled back into my warm bed. But Bessie needed to be milked, and Mother was in no condition to go out into the storm. After I'd bundled myself up, I lifted the door latch. The door swung open, and an avalanche of snow tumbled in. I fetched the enamel washbasin and scooped my way outside. I could see little farther than the red mitten on my outstretched hand. I had to get to Bessie. If she isn't milked twice a day, her udder will go dry in no time, and Mother needs the butterfat for her unborn baby. So I pushed into the wall of whiteness. Each step was a trial. My feet sank knee-deep into the drifted snow. With luck and an earnest prayer, I finally found myself at the door to the lean-to barn. The air inside the barn was nearly as snow laden as outside. If Bessie hadn't bawled, I might have mistaken her for yet another drift. Her coat was crusted with an icy mat of snow. Rufus and Mabel, looking quite like oxen ghosts, snorted steamy greetings from their nostrils when I forked fresh prairie hay into their stall.

Though I knew Mother would object, there was no question about what needed to be done next. I grasped Bessie's halter rope and led her outside. You've heard stories about how stubborn mules can be. Well, I am here to tell you that there is no creature on earth more stubborn than a cow who decides she is not about to be led into a blizzard, no creature save for me. I stumbled and tugged forward for what seemed an endless time, until my shoulder brushed against something solid. It was the corner of the soddy. A few inches to the left and I would have missed it altogether, led Bessie and myself out onto the open prairie. I shiver at the thought of our fate.

After groping my way along the wall, I found the door and led Bessie inside. Mother gasped, then said, "I'll not have a cow in my parlor." Though I didn't mean to be disrespectful, the trip to the barn had sapped my strength. "Hush, Mother, we can't have Bessie freezing to death." Mother shook her head, then plunged her hands in the mound of bread dough she was kneading. After I had warmed myself in front of the stove, I ventured out again, that time to unearth several bundles of prairie hay that Father had stacked around the foundation of the soddy. The hay serves as both bedding and food for Bessie. Seems I was going in and out all day, fetching wood for the stove and buckets of snow to be melted for drinking water — too dangerous to go to the well. And I made two quick trips to dispose of Bessie's dung. My bones are weary.

So here we are, your typical pioneer family: Mother knitting, me writing you this letter, Bessie chewing her cud, and a bevy of field mice, who moved in during the night, playing tag in the wood box.

As you most likely suspect by now, Father has not returned. He's been away nearly three months. Though I try not to worry, try to imagine him safe in a railroad camp, sometimes my imagination gets the best of me and I see him lying hurt somewhere, all alone. I pray for him.

December 1

Still no letup in the storm. My daily sojourns into the blizzard's fury have nearly worn me out. But our survival depends on me now, so I find the wherewithal to keep the coyotes from our door. Mother has grown silent, and cares are whittling lines upon her face. She rocks in her chair and stares out into the whiteness. It is a struggle for me to coax a few morsels of food past her lips. I worry so about the baby. If only Father were here! He would know the right words to pull Mother out of herself. Oh, Rachel, why hasn't he returned?

December 5

Glory hallelujah! I awoke to the bright face of morning — the sun is shining. Bessie is back in the lean-to, though it was a trial getting her there. She'd grown accustomed to her lavish accommodations. I coaxed Mother outside for a few minutes. The cold brace in the air served as a tonic for her spirit. She ate a hearty lunch of boiled potatoes. Father will surely come soon, now that the weather has cleared. He would not think of leaving us alone at Christmas. The tallow wick burns low. All for now.

December 8

No time to put a formal ending to these ramblings. J. Fowler is here. He traveled by cutter sleigh all the way from Prairie Hill to deliver the barrel Uncle John has sent. I'd like nothing more than to pry it open this very minute, but I don't want to keep Jess waiting. He is a generous man, has offered to take Mother and me back with him. But we cannot leave, what with Mother's time so near. I'll post another letter when I can.

Here's wishing you a joyous Christmas,
Abby

December 8, 1869

Dearest Rachel,

The bells on Jess's sleigh had barely faded when I pried open the barrel. Mother and I have been behaving like a couple of rambunctious children on Christmas morning. What a picture we must have made, Mother and I, holding hands, waltzing around that barrel. The ham, the apples, the pecans — oh, what a feast we will enjoy. The beautiful shawl for Mother, it lifted her spirits so. Why, she is even humming. And thank you for the rose-scented stationery, which reminds me so of Aunt Harriet's garden. If I'm not careful, the scent will be sniffed away before this day is done. That would be a shame because I have one more letter to write, a letter to Peter, a boldly romantic letter, thanking him for the silver thimble engraved with my initials. When next you see Peter, plant a kiss on his cheek and tell him it is from me. God bless all of you.

December 15

Mother's time has come. Her pains started in the night and have progressed ever so slowly. I am prepared. The kettle of boiling water whistles from the stove. Fresh linens are in readiness. I did as Mother asked and slipped the butcher knife beneath her mattress. She says the knife will help cut the pain. An odd gesture, but what harm can it do? Soon I will learn if I am to have a brother or a sister. I know, wherever he is, that Father prays for a son to carry forward the Chapman name. Mother calls, so I will close for now.

December 16

It's a boy! And I helped bring him into this world. Mother was very brave and cried out only near the end. She gave one last push, and there he was. I tied the cord with a length of string and snipped it with Mother's sewing shears. Then I bathed him with warm water and laid him in Mother's arms. He nuzzled her breast and commenced sucking noisily. He is a tiny little thing, not more than a few pounds from the feel of him, but he has strong lungs, and he uses them with great abandon. Birth is a miracle! One minute life was but a gleam in Mother's eye, the next minute I was cradling that life in the palms of my hands.

I am worried about Mother, though; she is very weak. I don't know what to do about the bleeding. I wish Aunt Harriet were here. She would know what to do, concoct some herbal remedy. I'm praying Mother will be stronger in the morning. I'm also praying that I will find the thimble Peter gave me. Though I have turned the soddy upside-down a dozen times, I'm frantic to find it, as I believe my stupidly losing it at this time is a bad omen. I must find it, tonight. I must.

December 18

Oh, Rachel, I need you, need someone, any-one, to be here with me now. I cannot do this alone. I cannot. I've prayed, asked God to undo the awful thing that has been done, but He has turned a deaf ear, abandoned me as

Father has abandoned me, us. I shook her, slapped her hard across the face, screamed into her ear, breathed my breath into her icy blue lips. But she's gone, beyond my reach. I want nothing more than to follow her, to go where she has gone, where Father has gone, where my beautiful thimble has gone.

December 19

Let it be known that a baby boy was baptized on this, the 19th day of December 1869. I, Abigail Esther Chapman, did sprinkle water upon his brow and did say the words "I baptize thee, Christian Albert Chapman, in the name of the Father, the Son, and the Holy Spirit." Let it also be known that a woman, Esther Abigail Chapman, dressed in her best navy woolen and wrapped in her wedding quilt, was laid to rest this day in a drift of snow five paces due north of the lean-to barn. Come spring, when the earth has thawed, she, we, would like to be buried in our meadow.

December 20

The snow comes again. The wind cries.

Bessie is close at hand, milk flowing for Christian. So innocent he is, so fragile. Caring for him, holding him, touching his flawless new skin, give me reason for hope. He needs a mother who is strong, so I will try to be strong. I will try.

December 24

Father burst through the door just before noon, laden with bundles. I thought him a ghost, covered as he was with a shroud of snow, icicles hanging from his beard. Words flowed, chantlike, from his lips, but they seemed foreign words. He grasped me about the shoulders and commenced to shake me. Christian began to cry. Father's head wheeled toward the cradle, then spun back to me. He renewed his chant. "Where's your mother? Where's your mother?" Meaning returned and awakened a beast in me. I went at him, fists hammering on his chest. "Where were you?" I shouted. "Why didn't you come?" He backed away and buried his face in his hands.

Oh, Rachel, Father refuses to hold Christian in his arms. When I offer, he turns away. How can this be? How can a man turn away from his flesh and blood? Christian is

his son, the son I can never be. Pray for us.
Pray for us all.

Abby

April 1, 1870

My dearest cousin Rachel,

We buried Mother in the meadow today, the
frost having given up its icy hold on the earth.
Finally Mother is at rest. Father fashioned a
marker from a wooden plank, on which he
carved "Esther Abigail Chapman, Our
Beloved Wife and Mother."

We are no longer alone here on the prairie.
Three German families arrived last week to
take up land adjacent to ours. Oh, how happy
Mother would be finally to have women
about. And I have a new friend. Her name is
Minna. She is only eight, but she is a dear.
Each afternoon she arrives at my door saying, "Teach Minna English words." In another family, there is a somber boy by the name
of Helmer. Though he is only twelve, his
father requires that he spend every waking
hour at the breaking plow.

Father speaks of moving on to the west to

try his hand at cattle ranching in the Nebraska sand hills. I've told him to go if he must, but I shall not leave. I cannot leave. I cannot leave Mother all alone in the meadow. I will stay here in this place and little Christian will stay with me. I will tell him of Mother and help him to know her as I came to know her. I will protect him, offer him my hand in the darkness, as Mother now does for me when the coyote howls in the night.

Abby

P.S. Tell Peter he is free from his promise to me.

Three

I wiped my eyes with the back of my hand, and then I slipped Abby's last letter into the side pocket of my backpack. This act was not a choice in the everyday sense; it was simply a thing I needed to do. Shrugging off a shiver of guilt, I retrieved my sketchpad and pencil from where they lay on the floor and quickly sketched the picture of Abby that her words had drawn in my mind. Her hair, to which I added only wisps of shading, cascaded over her right shoulder. Freckle dots peppered the bridge of her nose, her cheeks. Though I had no way of knowing if the image I'd drawn even remotely resembled the real-life Abby, this sketch pleased me in a new way. Drawing wasn't simply about seeing, but about feeling, too — the feeling I captured in Abby's eyes as they gazed down on the baby she cradled in her arms.

I folded the drawing and slipped it into the last empty envelope. I must have fallen asleep soon after because the next memory I have is of waking up to a room filled with sunlight. I squinted at the clock: ten-thirty. After rolling out of bed, I dug through the small suitcase, pulling out a faded green T-shirt and a pair of denim cutoffs, items I had purchased from a thrift shop. I was into grunge, but clean grunge. Sarah always ran these clothes through the wash three or four times before she let me wear them.

The kitchen table was set for one: bowl, silverware, paper napkin, and a box of corn flakes. Next to the bowl was a note:

> You were sleeping so soundly we didn't want to wake you. The milk and butter are in the fridge, and there's bread for toasting in the breadbox (be sure to unplug the toaster when you're done). Mom and I will be working in the meadow, and we are still hoping you will join us. To get there, follow the path that leads south from the barn, through the grove of trees. Scratch that. Mom just told me that they've had a lot of rain, and the old creek bed is muddy. Do this instead: walk to the end of the lane and turn south (right) on the gravel road. Cross over the bridge and keep walking for about a quarter of a mile (three city blocks). When you reach the gate, give a holler, and we'll find you.

The note was so Sarah — plan everything out, leave nothing to chance.

In the bathroom, which oddly was located off the kitchen, I undressed and stepped into Anna's "I have all the modern conveniences" shower. The shower base was a claw-footed tub. The plastic curtain hung from a halo rod above, and the showerhead was attached to a long rubber hose, the end of which was duct taped to the tub's spigot. Cleanliness, like many things on Anna's farm, was going to require extra effort. As I held the showerhead above me, I thought of Abby swimming in the creek, of Abby helping her father dig the well, of Abby bathing little Christian, of Abby in the meadow. *The meadow.*

I quickly toweled off, dressed, and returned to the kitchen, where I passed on the corn flakes, choosing instead a large square of the chocolate cake Anna had served for dessert the night before and a glass of whole milk, which was a treat. Sarah was into skim.

Outside, with my backpack slung over my shoulder, I headed down the lane. I was approaching the gravel road, my eyes cast down, always on the lookout for a new earth-find, when I heard the drone of a motor. I looked up just in time to see a rust red scooter turn in. Anna was steering, and Sarah was waving wildly from the seat behind. Four feet planted themselves in the dust when the scooter stopped.

Sarah climbed off. "Were you on your way to joining us?"

I nodded.

"I'm so pleased. But I'm afraid the meadow will have to wait. We've come back early so I can prepare a special lunch to celebrate your first full day here."

"That's okay," I said, then turned my attention to the scooter. It was old. I could tell this from the rust and from the shape, which was not like any scooter I'd ever seen.

"What do you think of my cool wheels?" Anna said, grinning. "It's a Cushman."

"It's swell," I answered, then gave her the thumbs up.

Sarah looked at me, at Anna, and then back at me. She was about to say something when Anna interrupted. "Sarah, why don't you let me make lunch? Then you can take Hope for a spin on the Cushman."

"Have you ever made stuffed mushrooms?"

"Can't say that I have."

"Well then, I guess the joy ride will have to wait."

Seeing my chance for some fun slipping away, I blurted, "Anna could take me." Then, realizing I'd sounded too eager, I added, "If you don't mind, that is."

"Of course I don't mind," Sarah said. But she did mind. It was there in her eyes.

If Anna saw Sarah's disappointment, she didn't let on. She kick-started the scooter, then shouted, "All aboard."

I climbed on, threw my arms around her waist, and we were off. Before Anna turned onto the gravel road, I glanced over my shoulder, expecting to see Sarah hurrying toward the house. She hadn't moved.

On the road, Anna opened the throttle up, and as we gathered speed, I leaned my head just far enough to the side to catch the full force of the wind, wind that carried as many flavors as Baskin Robbins: the lavender of a field of clover, the pine bouquet of a grove of trees, the spice of a barnyard; wind I'd later try to draw.

We had just passed the second intersection when the Cushman sputtered and died. "Out of gas," Anna said matter-of-factly. "Guess we'll have to walk home."

"Aren't you afraid someone will steal the Cushman?"

"Not much chance of that around here. Last time I ran her out of gas, she got home almost as quick as me. Lloyd Stuhr, who works my fields for me now, saw her standing alone by the side of the road. He loaded her in the back of his pickup truck and brought her on home. Time before that it was Eb Pinkney."

"Do you run out of gas often?"

"Seems so, doesn't it? I suppose if the walks home weren't so pleasant, I'd pay closer attention."

I thought about Sarah, who always stopped for gas as soon as the gauge reached the half-empty mark. *Sarah!* "We'd better get started or Sarah will worry."

"You were reading my mind."

As we walked, Anna told me the name of each farm we passed and the names of the people who lived there. Rarely were the names the same. Eb Pinkney lived on the Ernst Place, and Lloyd Stuhr lived on the Hembery Place, Ernst and Hembery being the last names of the original homesteaders. "It's our way of paying respect to the people whose hard work made our way of life possible," Anna said.

"Is your farm named after Abigail's father?"

A smile blossomed on Anna's face. "You read the letters."

"I did."

"I'm so glad, and the answer to your question is no. My farm is not named after Abigail's father. It's named the Schmidt Place, after my great-granddaddy. Shortly after Abby wrote that last letter, her uncle John came west, intent on convincing her father to return to Ohio. The two men quarreled, and the next day Abby's father signed over his homestead claim to my great-granddaddy, saddled up his sorrel, and rode off, never to be heard from again."

"What happened to Abby and the baby?"

"They returned to Ohio."

"How did you get the letters?"

"I'm saving that story for another day, but do you see those trees up ahead? Those are the cedars Abby kept alive. And this field of corn, that's the field she helped her daddy plow open."

"Is there anything left of the sod house?"

"No, those weren't built to last. Rain and wind and ice weren't kind to the soddies, though there's one still standing out in Custer County. Folks were living in it when Sarah was a girl. Fancied up a bit, with plaster walls and wood floors on the inside and a shingled roof overhead."

"When we get back, would you show me where Abby's soddy stood?"

"Sure, but like I said, there's nothing left."

"Maybe, maybe not," I said.

Sarah was waiting on the back porch when we arrived. "I was beginning to worry that you'd taken a spill."

"No spill," Anna said. "We decided it was a nice day for a walk."

"You ran out of gas, didn't you?"

"Mighty fine day for a walk. Is lunch ready yet?"

"Ten more minutes."

"Good. That's more than enough time to show Hope where Abby's soddy once stood."

Sarah turned to me. "Mom told me she gave you Abby's letters, and this must mean that you've read them."

I nodded.

"I remember reading those letters for the first time when I was a girl. Reading about Abby's life helped me better appreciate all that I had. Running water, electricity, a moth — "

Sarah's cheeks reddened. "How thoughtless of me."

"No problem," I said and meant it. Who better than me to understand the importance of appreciating one's mother?

"We'd better scoot," Anna said, "so we can be back in time to wrap our tongues around whatever it is that's giving off such a heavenly aroma."

Anna led the way across the yard, past the barn, the windmill, and between two tall tube-shaped buildings she called grain bins, before stopping at a low wooden shed.

"As the story goes, the old soddy stood right here, where the chicken coop stands today."

Anna opened the door, and I ducked so my head wouldn't knock against the top of the low opening.

"I haven't kept a flock of laying hens for several years now, so I've been using the coop to store some things."

"Nifty things," I said, brushing the dust off the seat of an old tricycle. "Sarah's?"

"Sarah's," Anna answered.

"Do you have a shovel?" I asked.

"Long-handled and short-handled, spades, hoes, and pickaxes, just about any digging tool you can imagine. Why do you ask?"

"I'm interested in archaeology, and I thought I might poke around here and see if Abby left anything behind. If I had some twine, I could mark off a grid, like they do at real dig sites, and keep a record of any artifacts I find."

"No problem," Anna said. "There's oodles of twine in the barn."

"Swell. And I'll need something to sift the dirt. Do you have any old window screens?"

"There are a couple gathering dust in the garage. You're welcome to them."

A bell clanged. We both looked up. The bell clanged again.

"Now there's a sound that stirs up old memories," Anna said. "My mama hung that bell on the back porch and used it to call us in for meals. Most farmwomen hollered their families to the table, but Mama, unless she was angry as all-get-out, thought hollering was unladylike."

The bell clanged again.

"On our way," Anna hollered.

We ate our lunch at the dining room table, which Sarah had draped with a linen cloth and set with gold-rimmed china plates. The sausage-stuffed mushrooms, balanced on a bed of wild rice, might have been delicious if I hadn't eaten that piece of cake. While I pushed my food around with my fork, Sarah and Anna chattered about their work in the meadow, something about a silo, but I was preoccupied thinking about my "dig." A dig of my own, one I wouldn't have to sneak into or out of.

After lunch, Sarah washed the dishes. I dried, Anna put away, and the half-dozen cats who had congregated outside the back porch licked the last remnants of my uneaten lunch off their whiskers.

"The meadow awaits," Sarah said, giving the tarnished faucets one last buff with her dishtowel.

I looked at Anna.

"You go on ahead, and I'll be there as quickly as I can," said Anna. "Hope's thinking she'd like to sift through the dirt where the old soddy once stood, see if Abigail left anything behind, and I promised to rustle her up some tools."

Sarah's smile slid off her face. "I was so hoping that we could all spend the afternoon in the meadow."

I was searching for the right words to help Sarah understand why the dig was so important to me when Anna said, "I have an idea. Why don't the three of us spend the afternoon in the chicken coop, getting it cleared out so Hope can dig."

"But the meadow . . . there's so much work to be done there."

"One afternoon isn't going to matter in the long run."

Sarah gnawed on her bottom lip, then said, "Okay, just this once."

A wave of disappointment washed over me. I'd always done my digging solo.

"I'm glad you want to help, but I don't want you to change your plans for me," I said.

"Nonsense," Sarah said. "Work is always more fun when it's shared. Let's make a list of the things we'll need."

"Shovels," Anna said.

"Stakes and twine," I added.

"A sledgehammer to drive the stakes."

"And an old window screen to sift the dirt."

"Something to balance the screen on."

"Sawhorses."

"A couple of lanterns. It's awfully dark in there."

"And a jug of lemonade."

Our first task was to clear all the stuff out of the chicken coop and transfer it to the "brooder house," which Anna explained was the place where each spring she had kept dozens of baby chicks. When the coop was empty, Anna went off to "fetch" one of the old window screens from the garage, while Sarah and I went to the barn to retrieve the shovels, sledgehammer, and twine. Entering the barn was like stepping inside a sad feeling. The air was dark, except for thin ribbons of light that threaded down from the cracks in the high roof. The air was still, except for the drift of dust motes stirred by our movement. The air was silent, except for the coo of a single dove. I was imagining how I might capture the scene in pencil when a cow mooed.

"I didn't know Anna had cows."

"Normally she doesn't, but Mom's cow-sitting for Eb Pinkney. His oldest son is getting married in Denver this weekend. One of the other neighbors is milking his dairy herd while he and his family are away, but two of his cows will be calving soon, so Mom offered to keep an eye on them."

"How soon?"

"Any day now," Sarah answered.

When all our tools and the lemonade had been collected inside the chicken coop, we marked off an eight-by-eight-foot square in the center of the dirt floor. Then Anna, after wrestling the sledgehammer away from Sarah, drove wooden stakes at each corner of the square and at two-foot intervals in between. Sarah and I strung the twine tightly between the stakes. The dig site was ready.

I placed the shovel blade against the ground, then positioned my foot on the blade's shoulder and pressed down. The earth resisted at first, but when I applied more weight, it gave way. A layer of dirt curled onto the shovel blade, and I carefully swung it over the screen, which was balanced between two sawhorses and stood just outside the perimeter of twine. Sarah and Anna watched while I ran my fingers through the dirt.

"Kind of like sifting flour," Sarah said, stooping to watch the filtered dirt sprinkle down from beneath the screen.

"Or the old-time way of separating chafe from grains of wheat," Anna added.

All I found in that first shovelful were pebbles. I wasn't disappointed. For me, archaeology wasn't just about the thrill of finding artifacts; it was as much about the anticipation of finding artifacts.

For a while, Anna and Sarah just watched. But I could tell by the way Sarah shifted her weight from one foot to the other, by the way Anna's body leaned forward each time I leaned into the shovel, that these women had no experience in being spectators of work.

"Dig," I said.

They dug.

Before long we had settled into a routine. Sarah and Anna, each with her own shovel, kept me supplied with dirt, which I sifted through the screen. The first earth-find was a nail, which Anna said was probably a nail she had stepped on as a girl.

The first real artifact, which arrived in a shovel dug from the second row, third square from the left, was a thimble. Though it was crusted with soil and looked just like another stone, I knew from the feel of it that there was some treasure hidden within. With my fingers, I crumbled the dirt away. The thimble was black, like the spoon hidden at the bottom of my backpack, so I guessed it was silver.

"I've found something," I said.

Sarah and Anna dropped their shovels and hurried over.

"May I see?" Anna asked.

I placed the thimble in her open hand.

"Look, there is some kind of marking here on the side, but I don't have my reading glasses on, so I can't make it out."

"Let me see," Sarah said.

Anna passed the thimble to Sarah.

"Looks like initials — A.C."

"Glory be," Anna said, turning to me. "Abigail Chapman. This is the thimble Abby wrote about in her letters, her gift from Peter."

Sarah placed the thimble back in my hand and closed my fingers around it. "You've done it, Hope. You've unearthed a piece of history."

All the other artifacts I'd ever dug up had belonged to nameless people, their lives only imagined, like characters in a novel. But that day I held a memory of a girl with a real story, a girl with a name — Abigail Chapman. This was a new kind of connection, one I hadn't known I'd been craving.

"Dig," Anna said, grabbing her shovel.

"Dig," Sarah echoed.

The last find of the day was a piece of broken comb, the kind women wear to hold their hair away from their faces. Anna found it. She didn't say anything. She just stood there, turning the pearlized comb over and over in her hand.

"What did you find, Mom?" Sarah asked when she looked up and saw Anna standing so still.

When Anna turned, her eyes glistened with tears. "This is a comb my mama wore when she first came to this place. It was part of a matching set. I have this comb's sister stowed in a box of Mama's things up in the attic."

"I remember that comb. Grandma Rebecca used to wear it whenever she wanted to get all gussied up. How do you suppose this one got out here, in the chicken coop?"

"Remember? Mama mentioned losing this comb in her journal."

"Your mother kept a journal?" I asked.

"Yes, when she was fourteen and newly arrived on this farm."

Another earth-find, another girl with a story. "Did you save the journal, too?" I asked.

Sarah laughed. "Mom's a one-woman historical society. If a thing finds its way here, it has found a home for life."

"Sarah is exaggerating. I only save those things that have memories attached to them, like Mama's journal."

"May I read it?" I asked.

"Sure. When we get back to the house, I'll rustle it up."

That evening, while Sarah and Anna visited over coffee with Lloyd Stuhr (he'd hauled Anna's Cushman home), I slipped up to Sarah's old room, where the journal was waiting for me. A few threads held the cover to the spine, and many of the pages lay loose inside. Fearing I might do more harm, I decided to read the journal sitting at Sarah's desk. With my sketchpad positioned at my left, the comb and Abigail's freshly polished thimble to my right, and my backpack at my feet, I began to read.

Four

24 June 1900

A good evening to you, little book. I will begin these writings by introducing myself. My name is Rebecca Randolph, and I am fourteen years old. Mum has given you to me as a parting gift. You see, tomorrow I am to go away. Papa has arranged for me to be employed as a hired girl on the Helmer Schmidt farm. Unbeknownst to me or Mum, he placed a farm-girl-for-hire advertisement in the *Prairie Hill Republican*. Mr. Schmidt was the only one to reply, writing that his woman, Minna, needed a strong girl to help her with the household chores. Papa is fond of placing ads. That's how he happened to marry Mum. He placed an ad in the London *Times,* asking for a strong Englishwoman to become his bride. That time Mum was the only one to reply. I was a wee thing, so I don't remember the ocean voyage or the train ride halfway across America. I wish I did remember. Mum said our trip was a fine adventure.

Mum is not in favor of my becoming a hired girl. Last night, pretending sleep, I heard her say to Papa, "Let her stay. Oh, please let her stay. There are things I haven't taught her, womanly things." Papa was not swayed. "I've shaken hands on it," he said, and I heard Mum's voice no more.

This evening, after she'd shooed Papa and the younger ones outdoors, Mum sat me down for our womanly talk. "You'll be needing these soon," she said, handing me a bundle of flannel rags. "When the time comes you'll know what to do." I wasn't sure I did know, but I nodded anyway. After the blush had drained from her cheeks, Mum slipped you, little book, onto my lap. "I'd give you the stars if I could, but for now this old journal of mine will have to make do. I've torn out all the written-on pages, so it's almost as good as new. If you write small, you can make her last until times are better and you are home with me again."

I wanted to tell her that her gift was better than a star, because it was something of hers, but Mum had said I wasn't to interrupt until she'd said everything she had to say. "Joseph's my husband, and I've no choice but to do what he thinks best. He took us in, you and me, even though I hadn't mentioned you in my correspondence to him. Less charitable men might have turned us away. He's always treated you like one of his own. You know that, don't you?"

I nodded, then swallowed the lump in my throat. "It's okay, Mum. I don't mind going." This was partly a lie. It is time I began earning my way, but I do have one regret. If I don't return to school in the fall, finish my studies, I won't be prepared to take the state teacher's exam when I turn sixteen. Perhaps this is for the best. Married women aren't allowed to teach. Though my teacher, Miss Epworth, has said I'll make an excellent teacher, I think I'll make an even better wife — to an upstanding and prosperous young farmer.

Mum has just told me I need to be getting off to bed, so I will close for now. When next I write in your pages, I will have begun my new life. Good night, dear little book.

25 June 1900

It has been the most trying of days. Papa chattered the whole five miles into Prairie Hill. Nervous talk about the weather, like I was someone he had just met, not the usual easy talk about the price of a bushel of grain or his latest scheme for getting out from under the debt he owes the Farmers and Merchants Bank. I nodded when it seemed fitting but said little. I was occupied by the ache of what I'd left behind — Mum's stricken face, the tears I tasted when I kissed Elizabeth and Eliza Jane's cheeks, the shy, boyish feet of Walter and George and Joey shuffling in the dust, and the feel of little Ruth's thin arms cinched about my legs.

Our arrival in Prairie Hill pulled me away from my thoughts, thoughts of any kind being hard to hold amidst the commotion that fills the town's sidewalks and streets. Wagons sped this way, carriages that, stirring up gritty clouds of dust that stung my eyes, which were all agog. A crowd milled about on the platform of the Burlington and Missouri Railway depot, like cows waiting at the barn door, impatient for the milking hand.

A few blocks farther south, past the Presbyterian church, the opera house, J. Fowler's Emporium, and the three-storied Butler Hotel, we reached the grassy town square where Papa tied his team to the hitching rail. There we waited, for nigh onto two hours, eating the lard sandwiches Mum had packed and watching workers lay one brick upon the other to form the cupola of the new county courthouse. What a magnificent building it is, looking for all the world like a castle where an English princess might live. I was about to ask Papa if we might peek inside when a farm wagon pulled up alongside our buggy.

Relief spread like morning sun across Papa's face. He leaped to the dusty street and offered up his hand. I didn't move. Couldn't. Not after I'd gotten a look at Helmer. He is a bull of a man, with a black beard that trails halfway down his chest and rises and falls with each raspy breath, and eyes as cool and dank as the root cellar on a moonless night.

Papa had to yank hard on my arm to get me to plant my feet on the ground. We stood there, Papa and I, beside the Schmidt wagon, me clutching my bundle of possessions, Papa keeping his hands stuffed deep in his trouser pockets. Helmer, making no move to unseat himself, eyed me in a way that made me feel that hoarfrost had collected on my flesh. Then, in a heavy German accent, he said, "Too thin. Girl's not worth ten dollars a month. For her I'll pay five."

"But, but," Papa sputtered, "we had an agreement."

"Five. And she's likely not worth that," Helmer bellowed back.

"Seven-fifty. I can't let her go for a penny less."

"Five dollars. Take it or leave it."

If a gust of wind had blown up about then, it would have whisked me away. That's how small I felt — knee-high to nothing. Papa rubbed his stubbled chin, then said, "Time to be starting for home. Work hard, Rebecca. Make me proud." Then, before unhitching his team, he whispered, "And remember to put a cork in that confounded curiosity of yours." A stone settled into my stomach as I watched Papa drive his team hard away and out of sight.

There was nothing left for me to do but to shove myself up and into the bed of Helmer's wagon, where I made a nest among the stacks of grain sacks. Helmer cracked his whip. I buried my nose in my bundle, which smelled of home — pipe smoke and liniment, talcum powder and babies and lilac-scented lye soap. As Helmer drove his team south on the dirt highway out of Prairie Hill, I made myself a solemn resolve. I would work hard, hard as a man if I must, to prove Helmer wrong, and I would be brave, brave as a wild crocus peeking up from under a blanket of late spring snow. Brave and strong, a credit to Papa. I would.

Dusk was settling in when Helmer finally whoaed his team. No sooner had his heavy boots thudded to the ground than he began to shout in German. A door to the house opened, slicing a wedge of yellow light across a small porch floor. A boy bounded out. Papa had made no mention of a son.

The boy led the team off toward the dim outline of a barn. Helmer took the porch steps two at a time, then disappeared inside. I licked the tips of my fingers, brushed back stray wisps of hair, and followed. I opened the screen door slowly and stepped into the kitchen. Shadows thrown from the flame of a kerosene lamp played in the corners of the high ceiling, and the darkness gathering outside pressed against the uncurtained window glass. The kitchen furnishings are sparse. There is no icebox, no cupboard, no sink, no pitcher pump, only a freshly blacked cooker, a small square table, and four caned chairs. No pictures or doodads hang from the walls.

Minna appeared so suddenly and quietly I bit my lip. She is a small woman, not much taller than I am, and she was dressed in black. Her drawn, dull face was framed by a coil of braid. But it is her eyes that visit me here in my little cot. They are nearly gray in color and as barren as a rosebush in winter.

She laid out the table with tin cups and plates, a pitcher of milk, and a platter of biscuits. My stomach rumbled, like far-off but coming-on thunder. Minna pulled out a chair and motioned me to sit. Sitting on the chair's edge, I folded my hands in my lap. Helmer, drumming his fingers on the table, stared toward the door. Minna fidgeted with a loose thread at the hem of her apron. From another part of the house a clock chimed. When the ninth chime faded, Helmer rose from his chair and strode to the door. "Otto," he shouted. We were waiting supper for the boy.

Otto burst through the door, plowing right into Helmer. Helmer raised his hand and struck Otto hard across his cheek. I gasped. Helmer's head jerked toward me. I thought he might come at me then, but he didn't. He drew in a heavy breath and clomped back to his chair. Eyes and shoulders slumped, Otto slid into his place at the table. Without the joining of hands, Helmer prayed a German prayer.

Helmer ate his three biscuits in the time it took me to nibble half of my one. He ate as one performs a loathsome chore — like emptying the chamber pots — a thing that must be done but from which one harvests little pleasure. When Helmer left the room, Minna turned to Otto and spoke hushed, German words. Otto rose from his chair and said, "Come, Ma wants me to show you where you will sleep."

I followed Otto and his oil lamp into the

dining room, which is even larger than the kitchen, though equally sparse. A sideboard huddles under the east window, and eight chairs wait at a long wooden table. Through a narrow gap in the oaken pocket doors, I glimpsed the parlor. Helmer, his spine stiff as a bed slat, sat in a straight-backed chair. The flame of his lamp was turned down so low I wondered how he read from what appeared to be a Bible.

After passing through the front hall, we climbed the open steps to an upstairs hall. Otto stopped halfway along, fumbled with the latch on a door, and mumbled German words. This sounded like cursing. When the door finally opened, we climbed yet another set of stairs, narrow and steep. At the top he plunked the lamp on a wooden crate and said, "You'll be expected up at half-past four." Then, like a firefly, he disappeared into the blackness below.

My cot is tucked under the slanting eaves, and inky windows at each gabled end seem to be watching me while I write. Near my cot stands a small chest of drawers. I undid the twine that tied my bundle and opened the top drawer. I was startled to find a silver-handled brush and a matching pair of pearlized combs. In the next drawer down were a nightshirt, undergarments, and a pair of cotton stockings. The bottom drawer holds a dress, neatly folded. The fabric is a fragile blue, nearly the color of forget-me-nots. How kind of Minna to provide me with these fine things. The only dress I own is a turned dress, made over from an old one of Mum's. She'd ripped it apart at the seams, sized the pieces down, then sewed them back together again inside out. There is but one thing missing — a pair of shoes. Mine have, this very day, begun to pinch my toes.

I hear a faint striking of that clock. Twelve chimes. Can it already be midnight? I must sleep, be ready for whatever tomorrow brings.

26 June 1900

I will tell you what I have seen and learned, but I must be brief so I get my sleep. My face is angry with me after a day's worth of stifled yawns.

The Schmidts are, as Mum would say, "bloody wealthy." No one told me this, but I have eyes. Helmer's barn is the largest and cleanest I have ever seen. Papa's barn would fit in its forenoon shadow three times over. The floor beneath the milking stalls is paved with brick and scrubbed so clean of manure one would not fuss if made to eat food right off it. The hayloft, which seems nearly as wide and high as the sky, cries out for a fiddler, a caller, and a dozen squares of dancers. Each of the many outbuildings Otto showed me is as neat and tidy as the next. An Aermotor windmill, a mechanical marvel made from metal, not wood, draws water into a large stock tank in the feed lot. Wouldn't Papa be proud to own one of those. His homemade windmill is forever giving him fits by breaking down.

Helmer owns three, yes, *three* teams of draft horses, plus herds of the healthiest-looking milk cows and swine I have ever seen. His machinery is of the most modern kind. Why, he even has one of those newfangled sit-upon plows. I plan to keep my eyes open, observe how Helmer goes about his work, so I might pass on some tips to Papa.

Only the chicken coop, where I sprinkled cracked corn for Minna's flock of Plymouth Rock hens, has been standing more years than me. An old soddy, that's where the chickens roost and lay their eggs. The Schmidts lived there until two years ago, when Helmer built the house. These are the only tidbits I was able to pry out of Otto as he showed me around the place. I don't know whether the bloke is barmy or just shy. Too soon to tell. But trying to talk to him is like talking to a tree stump. Well, that's not exactly right. A stump's story can be read in the width of its rings. Suffice it to say that Otto keeps his thoughts close to his union suit. I can only guess from the down on his chin and the wobble in his voice that he is some, but not much, older than me.

The house has not yet learned how to be a house. Instead of smelling like people, it smells of raw wood and sap. The floors don't even creak. Foodstuffs, crocks, dishpans, linens, a lard press, a coffee grinder, and a butter churn are stored in a small larder off the kitchen. Water is drawn from a hand pump out in the kitchen yard. This is not the most convenient of arrangements. Thirty steps separate the pump from the larder, twelve steps from larder to stove. On one of many trips back and forth, I counted.

After running my polishing cloth over the surface of the sideboard in the dining room, I pulled open each drawer and door to have myself a peek inside. Dwelling there are a set of gold-rimmed china dishes and crystal goblets that scattered tiny rainbows when I held one up to the window light. The grandfather clock, the one I heard chiming throughout the night, resides in the parlor.

The second story houses three large rooms. Otto's room contains a chest of drawers and a small cot, identical to mine. Nothing there gives me any clues to his character — no rock collections, no arrowheads, no horned toads living in jars. Helmer and Minna's room has one item worthy of note — a massive cherrywood bedstead.

The third room, the most awake room in this house, is not for sleeping. There is a rocker pulled up to the sunny, south-facing window, a New Home treadle sewing machine in a tiger oak case, a chin-high pine cupboard, and a quilting frame. Stretched within the frame is a half-finished quilt. Unlike Mum's quilts, this one follows no common pattern. On a field of white, Minna has appliquéd pieces of fabric that together paint a scene. A young girl sits by a tree-lined brook. If I'd had more time, I think I might have imagined my way inside, my sore feet dangling in the calm water, the breeze braiding through my hair. It is as pretty as a picture on a penny postcard. I hope quilting with Minna will soon appear on Helmer's list of my chores.

After sweeping the front veranda, I leaned on my straw broom and admired a stand of half-grown cedar trees. Like Minna's quilt stitches, they form perfect rows to the west and north. Whoever planted these trees must have been practiced in patience. Papa says cedars are the slowest to grow.

Minna is a puzzle. Though her English is nearly perfect, she spoke only when necessary, and not once did she flash a smile.

There is much more to tell, but I promised to be brief and my eyes whimper for rest. Until the morrow, my dear little book.

30 June 1900

I have neglected you, and for this I am truly sorry. My days are so filled with labor I have fallen into bed each night, asleep before my head dents the pillow. But tomorrow is Sunday, and Otto has told me, except for milking and feeding the stock, they do not work on the Sabbath. They don't eat either. After I have fed the chickens and gathered the eggs, I am to have the day off. And I must here admit, today, when no one was looking, I tucked a crust of bread into my apron pocket.

My vow to be brave has, like the skin on my hands, begun to blister. I do the work, everything Helmer scrawls on my daily list. My aching bones are proof of this. But the loneliness, thorny as musk thistle, pricks my heart. No one speaks, not to each other and not to me, except when I ask Minna or Otto a necessary question. It is as if words are time — a thing not to be wasted.

1 July 1900

I must begin by telling of the hurtful thing I did this day. After tending to the chickens, I returned to my attic room. Thinking we'd soon be heading off to church and wanting to please Minna, I slipped into the dress I'd found in the chest of drawers. It was a bit too roomy in the bodice and at the waist, but the length was right, midcalf. I brushed my hair, a full one hundred strokes, and pulled it back from my face with the pearlized combs.

When I stepped into the kitchen, Minna's face turned the color of ash. One hand covering her mouth and the other gripping the edge of the cooker, she swooned into a heap on the floor. Otto rushed to her side and helped her up and onto a chair. I ran outside, thinking I'd pump a dipper of water. Halfway across the porch, Otto caught my arm and spun me around. His eyes blazed, hot as cinders.

"What have I done?" I asked.

"The dress. It's my sister's dress, and you shouldn't have worn it."

"Sister? What sister? I didn't know you had a sister. Why didn't someone tell me?" My voice raced as fast as my heart.

The fire in Otto's eyes went out, and his hand fell away. "Eva," he said as if whispering a prayer. "It's been near a year now since she passed on."

Minna's black dress, her empty eyes — I should have guessed.

"I meant no disrespect. I thought the dress was put there for me to wear to church."

"We don't go to church. Not anymore. Pa says folks there are hypocrites, one hand pumping his, the other groping in his pocket for money." This was the longest string of words I'd heard him piece together yet.

Not wanting to pain Minna any more than I already had, I slunk around the side of the house and entered through the front door. As I tiptoed up the stairs, it occurred to me that I was wearing a dead girl's dress. Mum had burned all of Grandmum Randolph's things, so her spirit could rest. I got the feeling that Eva's spirit might not be resting, that she might be hovering about inside her dress. Once in the attic, I took it off quickly, smoothed out any wrinkles I might have made, and laid it out, peaceful-like, in the bottom drawer.

After a time, I crept down the attic stairs.

When I pressed my ear to the quilt-room door, I heard the sewing treadle rocking back and forth, as rhythmic as a lullaby. Helmer, who I hoped had just come in, sat in his chair in the parlor, reading his Bible. I headed straightaway for the barn, thinking the loft might be a fine place to spend the rest of my day off.

Hand over hand, I climbed the wooden rungs of the loft ladder. When my eyes were level with the floor, I froze. There, directly in front of me and leaning against a mound of straw, sat Otto, surrounded by dozens of doves. One was perched on his finger, and Otto was stroking its feathers and murmuring. I stepped lively down those ladder rungs.

Dodging cow pies, I followed a path south of the barn that aimed toward a stand of cottonwoods. Once in the grove, the moss-covered ground whispered under my feet. A twig snapped, and a red squirrel scolded me for disturbing its peace. I scolded back.

A little farther on, I happened on a creek with a swinging bridge strung from one bank to the other. Curious to see what wonder, worthy of the builder's labor, lay on the other side, I was drawn across. Upon reaching the middle, I stopped and looked down. Patches of light, which had threaded their way through the arch of branches, fell like gold coins upon the water's surface. A fish flipped out of the water, snatching up a dragonfly that had made the mistake of tarrying too long in one place.

I hurried to the end of the bridge, glad to plant my feet again on solid ground. The stand of cottonwoods on the south bank is thicker, darker, the kind of place where I imagine spirits might lurk. I ran, zigzagging through the trees, and burst into the bright light of a meadow.

Though the grasses are taller and the wildflowers more abundant, the meadow looks for all the world like Papa's north pasture. Arms outstretched, I whirled and twirled until I fell dizzily into the grass. As I lay there, watching wispy clouds float across the periwinkle sky, my thoughts went home. Mum was preparing her Sunday batch of raisin scones. Eliza Jane stood to the right of her, and Elizabeth to the left. Papa sat at the kitchen table, smoke curling up from his pipe, little Ruth gleefully bouncing upon his knee. Out in the yard the boys played a noisy game of kick the can. I hugged my knees tight to my chest, and for the first time all week, I let myself cry. I know this was childish of me, but there was no one about, no one to see, to hear, to care.

When my tears had spent themselves, a tiredness spread clean down to my bones. Later — it might have been a minute or an hour — I awoke to a rustling in the grass. I rubbed the blur from my eyes, looked about, but saw nothing. I hurried toward the creek. Reaching the bridge, I stopped dead in my tracks. The bridge was swaying as if someone had just crossed.

Back in the farmyard, I looked up to the window of the quilt room. Minna was rocking in her chair. In the barn, Otto was cooing with his doves. Tiptoeing past the parlor, I saw Helmer napping over his Bible. If not them, who? Eva? Eva's spirit? A chilling thought. I will think on it no more.

Oh, look what I've done. I've used up four more of your pages. What will I do when there are none left? In the future I must not ramble on so. Must be more miserly, make every word count.

2 July 1900

Helmer and Otto are putting up hay, so got up at four to help Minna with the milking. Scrubbed the milking parlor floor. Hoed in the garden. Churned. Butchered the supper chicken. Tuckered out. Will save the rest until Sunday.

8 July 1900

Visitors came to call on Tuesday — a Mrs. Ernst and her daughters, Ramona and Geraldine. Minna and I were in the wash house doing up the wash when Mrs. Ernst poked her head in and said, *"Guten Morgen."* Minna's back was to the door, but from where I stood I could see her face. Her eyes did a do-si-do in their sockets.

The girls stayed behind when the two women went into the house. I was glad for this. Finally, I might have chums to chat with. But I didn't want to be the first to speak, so I kept rubbing one of Otto's union suits across the ripples of the scrub board.

Geraldine, who is buxom and thick-hipped, jabbered something in German. My hopes burst, quick as a soap bubble. I kept on scrubbing.

"Oh, I forgot. Ma said Helmer found Minna an English girl this time," she said.

"This time?" I asked, the cork popping off my curiosity.

"He's hired three girls since Eva died. Not one of them stayed more than a month. The skinflint promised to pay two dollars a week, then found reasons why they shouldn't be paid — spilled milk, broken eggs."

Otto's union suit slipped beneath the water in the washtub and with it my hopes of winning Helmer over with my hard work, of getting Papa his ten dollars a month.

"Our hired man's woman does our wash," Ramona said.

I fished the union suit out of the water and began scrubbing, hard.

Geraldine shot a needle-sharp glance at Ramona. "Excuse my sister. If they gave medals for rudeness, she'd be first in line."

"Me? You were the one saying what an odd duck Minna is for doing up her wash on Tuesday," Ramona shot back.

"I wasn't being rude, just curious. Minna's the only farmwoman in these parts who does up her wash any day but Monday. Been doing it on Tuesdays ever since Eva died."

"How did Eva die?"

"She drowned in the creek on her way to the meadow. At least that's the story Helmer tells. Otto told a different story, at first. The day of the funeral Otto told his friend Charles Hembery that Eva drowned because she was running away from Helmer's razor strap."

The ring of rumor buzzing in my ear, I

asked, "How can that be? The footbridge?"

"There's no bridge, never was, never will be. It's not that Minna didn't try. She begged Helmer to build one, but he said he had better things to do with his time. He could have paid someone to build it, seeing as how he is the richest man in our district. Why, they'd still be living in that old soddy if folks hereabouts hadn't started to talk. And then he goes and shows everybody up by building the biggest house around. Those fine things in the house, the china, the crystal, those are Minna's, things passed down to her from her family. Helmer lets her use them only when it comes time to lay out the table for a crew of dirty wheat threshers. Rumor has it that he buries his money somewhere on the farm. Gold coins, mostly. Have you seen him? Have you seen him doing any digging?"

I shook my head.

"We are going to the Chautauqua Grounds tomorrow for the Fourth of July celebration," Ramona said, adding a pinch of bitters to the "we." "There will be bands and literary readings and operatic singers, and William Jennings Bryan, the famous Nebraska orator, is giving a campaign speech. He's running for president, you know. Everybody who is anybody will be there. Are you going?"

"Hush, Ramona," Geraldine said. "You

know Helmer never lets his hired girls go into town."

Otto's union suit sported a couple of new holes by the time the girls left.

The bridge. How it haunted me all through the week. Was it real or had I dreamed it? I went there today, straightaway after doing my chicken chores. The bridge *is* real, as real as this page upon which I write. Built from guilt perhaps, but crossable.

The meadow, which last week wore the lavender of the purple poppy mallow, had dressed itself in the yellow of the sawtooth sunflower. I lay down on the quilt I'd brought with me, but I didn't let my thoughts go home like last time. Instead, I shuttered my eyelids against the sun and imagined that the meadow was one of the English gardens Mum's so fond of describing. I was dressed in a yellow gown, a princess in waiting for her upstanding and prosperous prince. Soon, a pleasant warmth spread over my body. Letting go of all thought, I drew this warmth into the deepest parts of me. Slowly, like a butterfly emerging from its chrysalis and unfolding its new wings, I was filled and lifted up until I soared, reaching for a circle of brilliant white light. I wanted nothing more than to make my home inside this light, for-ever.

There was that darn rustling again, like last time, and when I opened my eyes I saw Otto just before he ducked into the trees. I called to him, but he didn't answer. Do you suppose that wretched chap was spying on me?

15 July 1900

Minna and Otto down with the grippe. Helmer has made no move to go for the doctor, so I've been doing my best to calm their coughs with herb tea and cool their feverish brows with damp face flannels. Helmer has been sleeping in the barn and taking his meals on the back porch. I wonder what he would do if I were not here. I wanted to go to the meadow today, to breathe in the light again, but I don't think it would be wise to leave my patients just now.

22 July 1900

Otto's fever broke on Wednesday, and he was mighty vexed to find himself starkers beneath his quilts. What was I to do? Let him wallow in his sweat-sopped nightshirt? Though he is up and about, his color has not returned, and he is still very weak. Yesterday Helmer stormed into the house and accused Otto of shirking. He said this in English, so I assume he intended it for my ears, too. If Otto's eyes had been bullets, Helmer would be dead.

Minna is also showing signs of recovery. Today, when I was bathing her, a tear ran down her cheek. I thought she was wishing I were Eva, a name she has called me often enough in her fever, but then she whispered, "Thank you, Rebecca." I wanted to hug her.

Though the dust has gone undisturbed, I've managed to keep up with the important work by increasing my pace and by rearranging things a bit. Have moved some of the foodstuffs and cooking utensils from the larder to the kitchen. When Helmer saw what I'd done, he got real jumpy, as though he'd swallowed a dozen live frogs, but he said nothing.

No meadow again today, but that's okay. I've learned to go there in my head. Until next week, my dear, healthy little book.

29 July 1900

Minna is much improved, in health and spirit.

She's fairly been talking my ear off. I can't count the times she's apologized for being so distant when I first arrived. Seems she'd grown fond of the other hired girls only to have their papas snatch them away. She'd figured I wouldn't last, either.

Otto, on the other hand, is up to his old spying tricks. With Minna's health improved, I'd stolen some time for myself in the meadow. The white asters were in bloom, and the air was alive with butterflies: monarchs, sulphurs, and swallowtails. Refreshed, I wended my way back through the cottonwood grove. Otto, his cap pulled over his blue eyes, sat with his back propped against a tree trunk. I tiptoed to within touching distance, then grabbed his shirtsleeve and tugged. "You're it," I shouted. He was awake, on his feet, and across the bridge in less time than it took me to remember how to laugh. I suppose I should thank him. It was the first good chuckle I've had since arriving here.

5 August 1900

Minna has been up and about since Monday. When she first saw the clutter in her kitchen, I expected her to tell me to put it all back.

Instead, she asked Otto to haul the whole larder cupboard into the kitchen. I offered to help, but Otto insisted he'd do it himself. He has more muscle than I'd thought.

Helmer wasn't so agreeable to this change. All through supper that night he stared at the cupboard. After he'd eaten his third helping of Minna's chicken and dumplings, he picked up his tin plate and pitched it across the room. The plate bounced off the cupboard and clattered to the floor. I braced myself. Otto swallowed loudly. Minna calmly folded her napkin, then picked up her plate and pitched it across the room, too. Her plate hadn't finished its wobbly, tinny spin when Helmer grabbed for the crockery bowl. "*Nein,*" Minna said, with a force that pushed Helmer back in his chair, his expression a stunned question mark. Minna pelted Helmer with a long string of German words. With each word, Helmer flinched, but never so much as when she said the only word I understood — *Eva.* At that, he broke for the door. He has not returned to the table for a meal since. It's not that he isn't eating. Minna leaves a full plate on the porch before we retire each night, and the next morning the plate has been licked clean. All this fuss over a larder cupboard. I wonder what will happen when Helmer sees the kitchen curtains Minna has stitched together from an old bed sheet.

Speaking of sewing, today Minna presented me with a new dress, cut from the same pattern as Eva's, but in a deeper blue. It fits perfectly. She also said she'd be honored if I wore Eva's combs to hold my hair away from my pretty face. There are so many questions I want to ask of Minna, especially about Eva, but I've restrained myself. I don't want her growing silent again. Losing her companionship now would be more painful than never having had it.

No meadow today, as it was raining, but I spent my afternoon in a place nearly as nice. Minna invited me to join her at the quilting frame. Otto, instead of spending his day in the loft with his doves or spying on me, went off to visit his friend Charles Hembery, whose papa farms the section to the east.

Until next week, my dear little book.

12 August 1900

Helmer's disappeared. Hasn't been seen since Wednesday, the first and only day I wore my new dress. I was on my way from the chicken coop to the house with my basket of eggs, fretting over having just lost and not been able to find one of Eva's pearlized combs, when Helmer stepped out of the barn. His head swiveled toward me, quick, as though I were the North Star and he the arm of a compass. After squinting for a long moment into the sun, which was at my back, he dropped his buckets. Milk spilled across the muddy ground. "Eva?" he shouted in a voice loud enough to wake the dead. "Eva?" he called again, starting toward me. His first steps were slow, careful, as if he treaded on ice, but as the distance between us narrowed, his pace increased to an awkward run. I should have dashed for the house, but the only thing on my mind was those eggs. If I ran, they'd break. So there I stood, clutching my straw basket to my breast when Helmer, the lines on his face gone soft, threw his arms around me and drew me heavily against his chest. "Eva, Eva," he moaned with each tighter squeeze. Eggy dampness spread down the front of my dress. Helmer shuddered, then let go and stepped back. The lines in his face turned brittle again when he saw that I wasn't Eva. "You?" he spat. "The trouble-maker." He lunged, knocking me to the ground. I scrambled to my feet, ready to run, but Helmer grabbed for me, catching the skirt of my dress. A hard yank, the sound of tearing cloth, and again I was on the muddy ground. Before I could squirm away, he'd dropped to his knees, pinning me down. I managed to get out one good scream before his hand clamped over my mouth. "It's time someone taught you your place," he hissed between clenched teeth. His hot breath smelled of hate. With his free hand, he fumbled with the buckle on his belt, all the while muttering German words. When the buckle finally fell free, I squeezed my eyes closed and braced myself, expecting the razor-sharp pain of the leather against my flesh.

"Nein, nein," a strong male voice shouted. I looked up. There stood a tall, muscular man, sighting down the double barrel of a shotgun, both hammers cocked. It didn't seem possible, but the man holding the gun, the man with the strong voice, was Otto. Though my body felt as limp as the cornhusk doll I'd once tried to bathe, I managed to get to my feet and move to Otto's side. "No more, Pa. No more," Otto said. Minna arrived a moment later, garden hoe in hand. Upon seeing Minna, Helmer let out a wail, then curled himself into a ball and began to weep. Otto jabbed the tip of the barrel hard into Helmer's side.

"Enough," Minna said. "Can't you see the man's broken? He won't be trying to hurt anyone, ever again. Let's go up to the house."

As if deaf to Minna's request, Otto pressed the butt of the gun firmly against his shoulder and recurled his finger around both triggers. "*Nein,*" Minna shouted just before the ornate hammers snapped forward. The air filled with a startling silence. Lowering the gun, Otto said, "There wasn't time to load the shells."

The three of us turned and walked back to the house. Once inside, Otto stood at the kitchen door, Minna and I at the newly curtained window. For a long time Helmer just lay there, his body a quivering lump. Then, as if he'd suddenly grown bones, he pulled himself up and into the shape of a man and staggered toward the section road.

Though Minna thinks Helmer will be back, full of repentance, the plates of food she leaves on the porch each night have gone uneaten.

I've been helping Otto with the outdoor chores, as there is too much work for one. Friday we birthed a calf. I held the mother cow's head, trying to calm her, while Otto reached down the business end and pulled. It's fortunate there is no field work just now, the wheat and hay having already been harvested. Come frost, I wonder how we'll manage the hand-husking of the corn.

18 August 1900

I have much to tell you, as it has been quite a week. On Tuesday, as Minna and I were pegging wet sheets to the line, Mr. Hembery raced his team into the yard. Otto, who was chopping wood nearby, reached the wagon just as we did. There in the back of Mr. Hembery's wagon sat Helmer, a rope coiled many times about his body, mud and feathers caking his beard. "Sorry I had to hog-tie him, ma'am," Mr. Hembery said, leaping down. "Found him in my hen house, wringing the necks of Hilda's chickens. Soon as he saw me he went wild, growling and thrashing like a badger caught in a trap. Took both me and Charles to pin him down. He's quiet now, but I wouldn't trust him any farther than I can spit. If he was my kin, I'd see about having him committed to that new mental hospital the state's built over Hastings way. Should have been done a year ago, from the stories I've heard."

"We'll be taking care of it," Otto said with an angry edge to his voice.

"Now don't go off half-cocked, boy. I'm

here to help. If you like, I'll haul him on into town myself, talk to Doc Kilgore or the sheriff."

"That's mighty kind of you, Mr. Hembery," Minna said, "but this is something we have to do ourselves. If you'll help Otto get Helmer out of your wagon and into ours, you can be on your way."

"Okay, but don't you go untying the rope."

"I won't."

The dust from Mr. Hembery's wagon hadn't settled when Minna began to untie the knot. "Otto, fetch the gun, and to be on the safe side, load it." Otto broke into a run. Turning to me, she said, "Rebecca, bring me a bucket of water, a cloth, and a hunk of lye soap from the wash house. When you've done that, go into the house and find Helmer a clean change of clothes. I'll not have him going off to a place like that looking like a filthy beggar."

Helmer looked almost normal by the time Minna had finished with him, except for the rope that bound only his ankles and wrists. And except for his eyes. No amount of soap and water was going to wash that empty stare away.

I helped Minna pack a food box while Otto hitched the best team of draft horses to the wagon, where Helmer lay on a bed of straw. When all was in readiness, Otto cracked the whip and the team pulled away. I stood there in the yard a long time after they'd gone, remembering the day I'd arrived. I'd been the one in the back of the wagon then, Helmer cracking the whip.

I was still standing there, lost in my thoughts, when a rider on horseback rode up the lane. After dismounting, the young man introduced himself as Charles Hembery. His papa, having seen Otto and Minna drive by, had sent him to do the milking. He has an upstanding look and is very polite. Charles came by both morning and evening the whole time Minna and Otto were away. Oh, how I wish I'd had my new dress to wear.

Minna and Otto arrived home yesterday just before dark. After I'd helped them unload the wagon and Otto had gone off to take care of the team, Minna said it was time she and I had a talk. We sat side by side on the bottom porch step. "The people at the hospital don't think Helmer will ever get well, say he's locked himself away in some dark place in his mind. This leaves me in an awful fix. First off, it's going to cost a pretty penny to keep him there, and we don't know where Helmer's buried his money. We'll start looking, first thing, but there's no guarantee we'll find any. Second, I've no money to pay your wage. Fond as I've grown of you, much as I'd like to have you stay on here, the day after tomorrow, Otto will drive you home."

Home: pipe smoke and liniment, talcum powder, babies, and lilac-scented lye soap; home: where every crumb of bread I ate would taste of Papa's disappointment. A tear betrayed me. "What is it, dear?" Minna asked, taking my hand. "I thought you'd be glad to be going home."

Otto joined us just then, and I told them about Papa's bad patch of luck, about the loss of his dairy herd, about his overdue loans at the bank, and about how much he was depending on my wages. When I was through, Otto rubbed his chin, the way Papa does, then said, "Do you suppose your papa'd agree to a trade, your wages for one of our best milk cows?"

"Oh, yes, I'm sure he'd be more than happy to trade me for a cow."

When we'd finished laughing, we started making plans. If we don't find some money soon, Otto will sell one of the teams of draft horses and the new-fangled plow. I suggested he place an advertisement in the newspaper, and he thought that was a capital idea.

So, dear little book, you can see why I said it has been quite a week. But it's not over yet. Tomorrow we will go to church. As the dress

Minna had made for me is beyond repair, Minna said she'd be honored if I'd wear Eva's dress, the one done up in forget-me-not blue. Remember how it was too roomy in the bodice? Well, when I tried the dress on today, I filled it out. Something besides corn has been growing on this farm this summer. Minna made me a gift of Eva's shoes, too. She says it's not proper for a woman to go barefoot, as I have been doing of late. This was the first time anyone ever called me a woman.

19 August 1900

After church, Minna invited Charles to Sunday dinner. Yes, Sunday dinner. And we ate at the dining room table, which Minna had asked me to set with the china and crystal goblets. Seated at the head of the table, Otto prayed an English prayer in which he thanked God for the usual blessings — bread, shelter, health, friends — adding an unusual twist before the amen. "And God be with us in our search for the money."

Charles entertained us with a detailed account of his recent trip to visit his grandparents in England. Imagine that, Charles is English, too. When Minna left the table to dish up the apple strudel she was serving for dessert, Charles turned to Otto and said, "There's a box social at the church next Friday night, and Ramona's been hounding me to find out if you're going to be there. If so, I'm supposed to tell you that she'll be baking your favorite butterkuchen and that you'll know which box to bid on because hers will be done up with a red bow."

Otto, his cheeks glowing the color of the imagined bow, turned his gaze on me. "I . . . I . . ." he stuttered. The poor fellow, that was all he could get out before Charles interrupted. "And Rebecca, might I ask what color ribbon your box will be done up with?" I looked from Charles to Otto, Otto to Charles, then lowered my eyes to my lap and said, "My box will be done up with red ribbon, too."

Now, little book, I must say good-bye. Your journey has come to an end here at the bottom of this last page.

Five

I sketched two images of Rebecca. In the first, two combs pulled her hair away from her face. In the second, I removed one comb, allowing an invisible wind to sweep wisps of hair, veil-like, across the right side of her face. The second sketch pleased me most. It gave Rebecca an air of mystery. It was like two faces: a brave face to show to the world and another, more private face hidden behind the veil.

It was after ten when I finished the second sketch, and because Sarah had already stopped by to say good night, I went looking for Anna. She wasn't on the roof, and her bedroom was dark, but light crept up the stairs, so I crept down. Anna wasn't in the kitchen, and no light bled out from under the bathroom door. I pulled a chair away from the table, wondering if it was the same table Rebecca had sat at the night she'd come to the farm. I imagined the tin plates and biscuits, the chime of the clock, the rush of air as Otto burst through the door. Otto? No, this rush of air was real. Anna was real. "I've just been out to the barn, and one of Eb's cows is going to have her calf tonight. Thought you might be interested."

"Cool," I said. "Should we wake Sarah?"

"Do you want to wake her?" Anna asked, lifting one eyebrow.

I thought about that. Once, when I'd been listening to the stereo with headphones, the volume set somewhere near max, I'd accidentally unplugged the jack. The speakers throbbed like giant hearts. By the time I got the volume turned down, Sarah was out of bed and stumbling through the doorway, shouting, "Duck for cover. It's a bomb."

"I don't want to wake her if you don't," I answered.

We entered the barn through a different door from the one Sarah and I had used in the afternoon. This door was smaller and split in the middle, so you could open either the top or bottom half or both halves at the same time. Once we were inside, Anna flicked on a light. To the right stood a row of wooden stalls. The first stall contained barn stuff, like straw bales and buckets, a wheelbarrow and empty burlap sacks. The next two stalls were occupied by black-and-white cows — Holsteins. "Dairy cows. Not walking T-bones, hamburger, and rump roast," Anna said. Each cow had a numbered yellow tag attached to one of its ears. The cow that was more black than white wore the number 568. The one that was more white than black wore the number 712.

"How is the mother-to-be doing?" Anna said as she entered 568's stall. The cow swished her tail as if in answer.

"Is there anything I can do to help?" I asked, hanging my backpack on a rusty nail that jutted from the wall.

"We need to get her on her feet so we can clean out the soiled straw she's lying on. If you get in front of her and pull on her halter, I'll push from behind."

The cow eyed me suspiciously as I approached her. "Nice cow," I said, feeling her warmth as I slid one hand under each side of her leather halter.

"On the count of three," Anna said. "One, two, pull."

The cow tried to shake me free, but I held tight; then, shifting her weight, the cow bolted to her feet. Her breath warm on my face, her round brown eyes inches from my own, she threw her head back with such force I had to let go of the halter. That's when I realized what a large and powerful animal she really was.

"Maybe I should hold her halter while you muck," Anna said. "The pitchfork is leaning against the wall over there."

Working quickly, I soon had the wheelbarrow overflowing. I then hoisted a fresh bale of straw into 568's stall. Using Anna's pocket knife, I cut through the twine binding, and the bale burst open. I sneezed, then forked the clean straw evenly across the stall floor. When I had finished, Anna let go of the cow's halter. Then 568 immediately lay down and breathed a sound through her nostrils that might have been a sigh.

"What next?" I asked.

"It's probably a good idea to have a bucket of water handy. We'll need clean hands if we have to help with the birth."

"Do we need to get the water from the windmill?"

"We could, but it will be quicker if you fill a bucket from that water spigot over there. My daddy installed running water in the barn the same year he installed plumbing in the house."

Anna's metal bucket was heavier than I'd expected. And once filled with water, it was almost too heavy to lift.

"Galvanized steel," Anna said when she saw me using two hands to carry it. "A plastic bucket wouldn't last long on a working farm."

Water sloshed down my legs.

"Would you like a hand?"

I nodded, and Anna relieved me of half of the bucket's weight.

"Now all that's left for us to do is wait," Anna said when we'd set the bucket down.

The cow shifted, then breathed out a different sound, not a sigh or a moo, but more like a strained bellow.

"What will we need to do when the calf actually comes?"

"Hopefully nothing. It's best not to interfere unless something goes wrong."

"What can go wrong?"

"Lots of things. The most common problem is that the calf can come out tail-end first instead of head-end first, which means we'd have to help by pulling."

"Doesn't that hurt the calf?"

"The calf usually survives, but sometimes, especially if the person doing the pulling isn't extremely careful, the mother can suffer internal injuries and die."

Cow 568 breathed hard. Her belly heaved. She lifted her head and looked at us.

"You're doing a fine job," Anna said, and the cow laid her head back down.

Anna turned to me then. "Have you ever sat on a straw sofa?"

I shook my head.

"Let's build one then."

The first bale, we shoved against the wall. The second, which would become the seat, we shoved against the first, and the third, against which we would rest our backs, we stacked on top of the first.

Our sofa was comfortable, in a scratchy sort of way. "If we stacked two over two, we could make a table," I said.

"And three over three, a bed," Anna added.

"And — " Cow 568 interrupted with another bellow, as if to remind us why we were sitting on a straw sofa in a barn in the middle of the night.

Anna and I were both quiet after that, sitting and staring at the rise and fall of the cow's belly, as if we were watching a black-and-white TV. Sitting and staring until, if the poor cow had been me, I'd have wanted to scream.

I turned to Anna and asked, "How long do you think it will be?"

"You can never be sure, but I'm guessing it might be another hour before the big event."

"I was thinking maybe we should give the cow a privacy break."

"She might appreciate that. Would you like a tour of my barn?"

"Lead the way."

The first place Anna showed me was the "milking parlor," where cows had lined up twice a day, every day, to be milked — in the early years by hand, later with electric milking machines. I imagined Rebecca there, scrubbing the brick floor or, working alongside Otto, balanced on a three-legged stool, milk squirting musically into a galvanized steel bucket.

The section of the barn Sarah and I had walked through in the afternoon looked very different with the lights on. Objects that had only been shadows took on recognizable forms. Lined up along one wall were some of Anna's farm implements. She told me the name of each and explained its use. There was the 1936 John Deere tractor, which she promised to teach me how to drive, the hay rake, the harrow, and the six-bottom plow. She said she had more implements stored in other buildings around the farm, and that she kept them all in working condition, just in case a younger person might want to use them someday. She winked at me when she said that. For a moment, I let myself imagine what it might be like if that person were me — mucking out stalls, milking cows, and planting perfectly straight rows of corn.

Anna stayed below when I climbed the wooden ladder to the hayloft. Empty, except for a flutter of dove wings, the loft was as big as a roller rink or a basketball court or, with the help of an imagined skylight, an artist's studio and garret.

"Say something," Anna called up.

"What should I say, say, say?" I asked, my voice echoing back many times.

"Hope," I said. "Hope, Hope, Hope," I heard. I

said "Hope" again, then "Anna" before the last "Hope" faded away. Then "Hope, Sarah, Anna, Rebecca, Abby, Abby, Abby."

"Sounds like all the young women of this farm are up there with you," Anna said.

I quickly climbed down. "Do you think we should check on 568 now?"

"I was just thinking the same thing."

Back at the stall, Anna lifted 568's tail. "Won't be long now."

We sat on our straw sofa and stared again, but I didn't sit for long. The cow made the strained bellowing sound again, and just like that, the tips of the calf's front feet peeked out. I dropped to my knees to get a better look. When the straining stopped, the feet disappeared. I turned to Anna. "Is something wrong?"

She shook her head. "Everything's going according to nature's plan."

The birth was like the moon on a partly cloudy night — hiding, showing, then hiding again. Feet, no feet. Nose, no nose. Eyes, no eyes. Head, and then, with the final strain, 568 delivered a glistening bundle into the straw. The calf, which seemed all head and legs, didn't move, didn't seem to breathe.

My head whipped toward Anna. "It's not breathing. Shouldn't we do something now?"

"The mother knows what to do," Anna answered in a calm voice. And she was right. The cow reached around and began licking her baby. She licked and licked, and suddenly the calf sucked in a breath, then a second and a third, and stretched its spindly legs for the first time.

"This is so cool," I whispered, not taking my eyes off the wiggly black-and-white miracle. "What happens now?"

"The baby's not out of the woods yet. Its mama has to lick it dry. Then, sometime in the first hour, the calf needs to find its legs, stand, and suckle the nutritious first milk from the udder. We'll need to stay until all those things happen, but one of us will have to keep talking or I'll fall asleep sitting up," Anna said through a yawn.

My stomach knotted. Leading conversations, especially late-night conversations, was risky. Once, when a foster mom had caught me sneaking into the house at 2 A.M., I'd let down my guard and told her about my dream searches, told her I believed, if I could find the dream field, my mother would be there, alive. All the conversation had gotten me were six months of weekly sessions with a counselor, who had spent the entire time trying to convince me to open my backpack for her.

"What would you like to talk about?" I asked as the calf opened one eye.

Anna chuckled. "It doesn't work that way. You'll have to ask me a question, get me started."

The cow was still licking, still nuzzling. "Okay. How long does the calf get to stay with its mother?"

"This one's lucky. She'll get to stay with her mother until Eb gets back from Denver at the end of the week."

That didn't seem lucky to me. It seemed cruel and sad, but I didn't want to say that to Anna because she'd been a farmer. Instead I asked, "How long before this calf is old enough to be milked?"

"Until around the age of two, all she has to do is be cute and eat. After that, she'll have to earn her way."

"Like Rebecca had to earn her way."

"Something like that."

"Did Otto trade Rebecca's papa a milk cow for her wages, or did they find Helmer's gold?"

"Paid him in milk cows, two each year until Rebecca's papa had built up a new, healthy herd."

"So they never found the gold?"

"The answer to that question is all tangled up in another story. My story."

I turned to Anna and lifted one eyebrow. "Your story? Did you keep a journal, too?"

"No, I've always been more of a storyteller than a storywriter, though Sarah has been after me to tell my story to a tape recorder. I tried talking into one of those contraptions once, but when my voice came back out, it sounded more like a hen cackling than it did like me. Besides, I can't tell my stories unless I have a living, breathing audience."

"Does one very interested girl, two cows, and a newborn calf, all living, all breathing, make an audience?"

"Add in a couple of doves and a barn cat or two, and there's no stopping me."

The calf was trying to coordinate its new legs into a tippy stand when Anna began.

Six

My story begins on a June morning in 1936. I was having a dream. I don't remember the particulars, but it must have been pleasant because of how irritated I felt when Mama's voice shattered it to smithereens.

"A-n-n-a!"

Mama had a habit of raising the pitch on the last *a* when she was annoyed, so I knew I was in trouble already, and the day had just begun. I flopped a hand into emptiness on the other side of the bed. Jane, my sister, was already up. Perfect Jane. I was convinced she rose early just to make me look bad. Before that summer, I'd been an early riser too, my eyelids winking open at the rooster's crow, anxious to see what adventure the day held. But all that had changed with the arrival of my bosoms. They'd popped up that winter, and I wasn't too keen on them. At first I'd tied a tea towel around my rib cage to flatten them. No luck. They had a mind of their own.

My bosoms were like red flags to Mama. Before they'd erupted, she'd pretty much let me do whatever I wanted. When my chores were done, I'd been free to tag along behind Daddy and Henry, fish for bullheads in Beaver Creek with my best friend, Jimmy Foster, and do anything my heart desired. But that summer Mama was gripped with the notion that it was high time I became a proper young lady, a replica of Jane.

"A-n-n-a," Mama called again. "Get your lazy bones out of bed this instant."

My feet hit the floor with a deliberate thud, and I was glad Jane wasn't in the room when I worked my cotton nightshirt up and over my head. All that summer she'd been trying to sneak peeks at my chest. Saturday nights, after she'd taken her weekly bath, she'd linger in the wash house and chatter on about the latest radio episode of *Fibber McGee and Molly* she'd listened to over at Bucky Baker's house. I'd wait her out, which usually meant I had to heat another boiler pan full of water to add to the soap-scummed water in the galvanized tub before I could undress and slip in. Though she was seventeen, four years older than I was, Jane's chest was as flat as a couple of fried pullet eggs, sunny-side up. If she'd known for sure that mine were already larger than hers, she would have had a conniption fit.

I rummaged through my bureau drawer and snatched out a pair of faded dungarees and one of Henry's old white shirts. Henry was my brother, younger than Jane by a year. We'd been friends

118

once. But since my bosoms, he didn't talk to me much. I'd found the shirt in the rag bag and thought it perfect. I tied the tails together at the waist and rolled up the sleeves past my elbows. In front of the vanity mirror, I ran a brush through my brown, bowl-cut hair, then turned from side to side and studied my reflection. A great disguise!

I smoothed the star quilt over the rumpled bed sheets and patted down the lumps. Mama had a fixation about unmade beds — one of many fixations she had regarding tidiness. Personally, I couldn't see the point to all the fuss. Jane and I would rerumple the sheets when we climbed into bed that night.

The grandfather clock chimed its sixth and final chime as I shuffled into the kitchen. Mama, who always rose promptly at half past four, looked up from the kettle she was stirring, made little *tsk* sounds with her tongue, and said, "Just look at you. You look like one of those old hobos."

Mama hated hobos. Our farm had been crawling with hobos that summer. They'd hop off the freight trains that ran smack through the center of our land and rap on our kitchen door, asking whether they could sharpen Mama's scissors or chop some kindling for her cook stove. Mama always gave them a hunk of her home-baked bread and a Mason jar filled with water, then closed and latched the door.

The hobos fascinated me — men moving on

from place to place, seeing things, doing whatever they were of a mind to. I'd given some thought that summer to hopping a freight train myself. But I'd never worked up the courage. Besides, I'd never seen a girl hobo.

Jane, who was darning a hole in the heel of a sock, looked up when I pulled my chair out from under the round oak table. In her best nasal whine, she said, "Mama, Anna isn't wearing her brassiere."

The word *brassiere* grated on my ears, the same way that the contraption Mama had ordered from the Montgomery Ward catalog grated on my shoulders and ribs. I was about to casually mention how at least I didn't have to stuff mine with quilt batting, when I decided it was wiser to let that topic rest. I slumped over my bowl of congealed cornmeal mush.

"Sit up straight, Anna, don't slouch," Mama scolded.

A quick escape was my only hope, so I started to wolf down the gruel.

"Anna, where are your table manners? Proper young ladies eat slowly."

The screen door creaked open, and Daddy, dressed in his bib overalls and denim cap, poked his head into the kitchen. "Rebecca, have you seen my long-handled shovel? Elmer Hackbart's offered to pay me in cash if Henry and I dig him a new outhouse pit."

Mama slowly wiped her hands on her apron, which she always did when she was thinking, then asked, "Have you looked in the woodshed?"

"Not there," said Daddy, stroking his beard.

"The granary?"

"Not there either."

I had to shovel a spoonful of mush into my mouth to keep from giggling. Mama had been night digging again. She liked to believe that her digging was a secret, but we all knew. The evidence was everywhere — holes among the cedar shelterbelt, holes in the front lawn, and holes even under the veranda. In years past she'd taken the time to fill those holes back in. But that summer, with money as scarce as rain, her digging had become more frenzied and she more careless. There wasn't one of us who hadn't nearly broken an ankle stepping, unawares, into one of her holes.

Mama, her hands still tangled in her apron, looked like she was about to suggest another place for Daddy to check when her eyes swiveled toward me.

"Anna, didn't I see you with the shovel yesterday?"

I stared back at her. I had used the shovel to bury the crow Henry had shot with Daddy's old-time shotgun. But I'd been extra careful to lean the shovel against the wall in the woodshed, the exact same spot where I'd found it.

"I always put the shovel back," I said, leaning hard on the "I."

"Don't use that tone with me, young lady. If I find out you're lying, you can forget about going into town Saturday night."

Daddy didn't leap to my defense the way he once had. Instead, he let the echoing thump of the screen door speak for him. For three summers straight there'd been no rain, and for three summers straight his crops of corn, winter wheat, and rye had shriveled to stubble in the fields. The soil was so thirsty it had split open in jagged, crusty plaques. Then along came the wind, which sucked up the topsoil and blew the most fertile parts of our farm to who knew where — Canada, maybe. What we got in return was a blanket of worthless, red clay dust blown in from Oklahoma. Even the old-timers couldn't remember such a long, dry, hot spell. Daddy's mood had grown more sour with each sun-filled, one-hundred-degree day, each day the taxes had gone unpaid. I'd taken to avoiding him, the way one avoided a house that had been quarantined because of scarlet fever.

"Speaking of missing things," Jane said, "I hung my blue dress on the clothesline yesterday, and when I went out to fetch it, it wasn't there. Anna, did you take my dress off the line?"

I cupped my hand and tried to catch a fly midair. "Maybe the grasshoppers ate it."

Mama wagged her finger at my face. "Anna, did you do something with Jane's dress?"

"Why do I get blamed for every little thing that goes wrong around here?"

"Anna, don't sass."

My throat squeezed up, and tears stung my eyes. Tears were another thing that had showed up with the bosoms. I'd always had a tough-as-nails constitution, never cried, not even when I slid down the haystack and gored my thigh on the rusty pitchfork tine. But that summer I found myself bursting into tears over the silliest things.

"Anna, don't be such a bawl baby," Jane said.

"Leave her be, Jane," Mama said, resting her hand on my shoulder and giving a gentle squeeze. "When you were Anna's age, you'd have thought you were slicing onions twenty-four hours a day."

Mama was like that. She'd be right in the middle of giving you the dickens for something, and then, as if a window shade had lifted, letting in some sun, she'd do or say a kind thing. I wiped my eyes with the back of my hand and focused on my blue-specked enamel bowl. I was scraping the bottom when the shade was lowered again with Mama's announcement. "By the way, the ladies from the Quilting Guild are stopping by at ten."

The mush curdled in my stomach. A parlorful of Mama's friends was almost harder to bear than bosoms. I remembered the last time the guild had congregated at our house for their quilting. Mama had made me and Jane recite a Bible verse. I'd say a line, then Jane would say the next. It began, "To everything there is a season and time for every purpose under Heaven." Jane had sparkled from the attention, like Mama's gold-rimmed Haviland china, which she set the table with only when company was invited to Sunday dinner. Putting on airs was Jane's cup of tea, not mine. I was who I was — an everyday, slightly dented tin plate.

"Ramona Baker's not coming, is she?" I asked, remembering how her eyes had marched up and down my body before coming to rest on my chest.

"Of course she is," Jane piped up. "When I marry Bucky, Ramona's going to be my mother-in-law."

Jane didn't see Mama roll her eyes, but I did. Not liking Mrs. Baker was one thing Mama and I still agreed on.

"We'll see about that," Mama said to Jane before turning to me. "In the meantime, Anna, it wouldn't hurt you to put on a dress before she gets here. I don't want Ramona starting any rumors about you being unladylike."

"Who cares what that old biddy thinks?"

"You'll care if she decides to ruin your reputation."

"Anna won't need any help ruining her reputation if she keeps arm wrestling with Jimmy Foster," Jane said.

Mama raised an eyebrow. "What's this about arm wrestling?"

I decided it might be wise to take a positive approach. "I won four times out of five."

"And where did this arm wrestling take place?"

Jane giggled, then said, "In the barn."

I kicked at Jane's leg under the table. "What's wrong with that? Jimmy and I have been playing in the barn since we were old enough to walk."

"You're getting too old for playing. As of right now, you won't be seeing Jimmy again unless you are in the company of adults."

I stood up so fast that my chair tipped over. "You'd better ask Jane what she and that pimple-faced Bucky were doing in the hayloft, then. They're the ones who need chaperones, not me and Jimmy."

I didn't wait around for Jane to tell Mama I was lying, which I wasn't. Instead, like Daddy, I let the screen door tell them both what I was thinking — thud th-thud — then raced across the yard.

Time in the meadow was the thing I needed, but Mama, in a tizzy over all the hobos traipsing about, had forbidden me to go there that summer. I counted out the risks as if they were coins and decided that spending them on the meadow was worth it.

If I'd had my wits about me, I'd have taken

the easy route — sneaked down the lane to the dirt road, crossed over the wooden road bridge, and entered the meadow through the stock gate. But I was in a mighty big hurry and settled on the straight-as-the-crow-flies path through the cottonwood grove that lined the banks of the creek. Crossing the creek wasn't a problem because I used the swinging bridge, even though I could have walked across the creek bed itself. It had been bone-dry since early June. The problem was the barbed wire Daddy had strung around the meadow to fence grazing sheep in and trespassers out. He called it a pasture. I preferred the word *meadow*. It was more poetic, more fitting for such a lovely place.

There were two ways of dealing with the mean-spirited wire. You could shimmy under the bottom string of barbs or climb over the top. My new body shape had eliminated the first option, so I grabbed the top wire and pushed down. I'd have made it, too, if I'd lifted that last leg a tad bit higher. My hand came back bloody when I reached around and felt my bottom. I thought of returning to the house to have Mama paint iodine on the gash, but I decided facing her at that moment carried more risk than lockjaw.

Stepping out from under the musty shade of the cottonwoods and into the meadow was like stepping into a painting. Black-eyed Susans splashed yellow and prairie roses dabbled pink across a canvas stroked by the tall green grass. The other plant life in the countryside had been scorched to a rusty brown, even the wiry weeds, but the meadow was different because it had never been laid open by a plow. The grass's roots fingered so deep into the soil, where the ground water had gone to hide, that they were nearly drought proof.

But this didn't account for the fact that the grass was taller than I remembered ever having seen it. *Sheep.* That was the answer. Summers before, Daddy's herd of Staffordshire sheep had grazed there, like a hungry threshing crew. Daddy'd had to sell off the sheep. Left alone, the prairie grass and wildflowers had returned to their natural, glorious form.

In years past, I'd whiled away much of my free time in the meadow. When I was younger, I'd shared it with Henry. He'd hammered a fort together from old boards and liked to play cowboys and Indians. He was always the cowboy. I was always the Pawnee princess. I'd wanted to be Annie Oakley — the name was nearly right — but Henry was the one with the cowboy hat and the hand-carved wooden pistols. In the last few years, though, he'd been too busy for playing. Daddy was training him to become a farmer. We'd had family picnics in the meadow, too, before Mama and Daddy got all wrapped up in surviving the drought.

I headed toward Henry's old fort, where Jimmy and I often met. I hadn't gone far when I nearly stumbled over a dark heap nestled in the grass. Stepping back, I studied the shape and settled on the notion that it was a body, a human body, most likely a hobo. He was dressed in a blue work shirt and denim overalls, the kind of garb Daddy always wore, and his face was hidden beneath a sweat-stained felt hat.

I knelt in the grass and watched the chest for signs of breathing. None. I tugged on the sleeve. Nothing. It dawned on me then that the hobo was dead. One more poke for good measure. My finger touched flesh, and a gnarled hand shot up and grabbed my wrist. I tried to scream, but the air I needed to make the sound stuck like a fly to fly-paper in my thudding chest.

"Don't be frightened, dear. I'm just an old woman who lay down to rest her weary bones," the hobo said in a thin voice. She let go of my hand, removed her hat, and sat up.

My mind had to switch directions, the way it does when you gulp from a glass your tongue thinks is filled with water, only to quiver at the taste of lemonade. Not for a minute had I expected the body to be that of a woman.

Her hair, which was pulled back into a tight

bun, was the color of Christmas snow, and her face bore the wrinkles of someone who has lived a long, long time. She had the saddest eyes, round and dark, like cow eyes.

"Peaceful here, isn't it? I took rambles here when I was a girl about your age."

"You lived here?"

"Indeed! The land was virgin prairie for as far as the eye could see. I hardly recognize it now, what with all the changes — roads and fences and railroad tracks and barns and silos and white frame houses."

Then, gazing into my eyes, she asked, "Does your mother come here with you?"

"Not for a long time."

"That's a pity. My mother is here."

"What do you mean?"

"Here in the meadow. Buried just over there. I've been telling her about my life."

I decided in that instant that the old gal was crazy, probably an escapee from the Nebraska State Hospital over Hastings way. There was no body buried in my meadow. All the dead folks were safely and *silently* buried in the Prairie Hill cemetery. I was about to hightail it out of there when the old woman rested her hand on my knee.

"The spring after Father and I buried Mother here in the meadow, my uncle John arrived unannounced and spirited me back to Ohio. I begged him to let me stay, but he left me no choice. He said if I didn't go with him, he'd take my boy away. I vowed on Mother's grave that I'd return one day. And that day has finally come."

I conjured up a mental picture of the map that pulled down over the blackboard in our one-room country school. Ohio was east, on one of those big lakes. "You've come all the way from Ohio? How'd you get here?"

"Walked mostly, though I rode the last little way in a Burlington and Missouri boxcar. I watched how the hobos did it, and when no one was looking, I climbed up."

There were woman hobos after all. I had stumbled on something quite exotic.

"Does your family know where you are?"

"All gone, save for me. My boy, Christian, anxious to prove himself a man, went off to fight in the Spanish-American War and got himself killed in Teddy Roosevelt's charge up San Juan Hill. Uncle John and Aunt Harriet have been at rest for nigh onto twenty years, and I've spent these last few years nursing my cousin Rachel and her husband, Peter. But they're gone now, and I've come all this way to be with Mother in the meadow."

"What about your daddy? What happened to him?"

"He took to the drink after Mother passed on. When Uncle John came west to fetch me, he and Father quarreled. The very next day he signed over his homestead claim to a family of newly arrived German immigrants, saddled up his sorrel, and rode off. I never heard from him again."

"Your husband?"

"I never married, though not from lack of fellows asking. Jess Fowler, the young man who ran the Prairie Hill store back in those days, got wind that I was to return to Ohio and asked my uncle for my hand. If the deciding had been left up to me, I would have said yes. Though he was a bit rough around the edges, Jess was a good and generous man. Marrying him would have meant Christian and I could have stayed on here, close to Mother. But Uncle John ran him off, saying I was too young to get hitched. Too young. Imagine that. I lived more in that one year on the prairie than some folks live in a lifetime."

"Who else asked you to marry him?" I asked, not wanting the storytelling to end.

"Peter. He was the boy I was sweet on before I came west. We'd made plans that he'd join me in Nebraska when he turned eighteen, that we'd be married and take up a homestead of our own. But the Abby that left Ohio wasn't the Abby that returned. I had my boy to care for, and Peter took no interest in him. What interested him, I eventually saw, was my cousin Rachel. They married a few years later, with my blessings."

"Won't Rachel and Peter's children wonder where you've gone off to?"

"Sadly, though I delivered hundreds of babies in my fifty-odd years as a midwife, I never had the pleasure of delivering a baby for Rachel."

"Tell me more." I hoped if I kept her going, she'd answer the question that was begging to be asked: if she'd never married, then who was the daddy of her boy? Jane had told me, in her haughty, know-it-all way, how babies got made, so I knew Abby hadn't plucked that baby out of her mama's cabbage patch.

"Enough about a witless old woman. I want to know more about you, want to know your story. I've been watching you these last couple of days going about your chores, so I know you have strong arms, know you're not afraid of getting your hands dirty with old-fashioned hard work."

My cheeks grew hot as I quickly reviewed my comings and goings of the last couple of days, but they cooled again when I decided I'd done nothing to be ashamed of. "I don't mind work, if it's outdoor work. But I'm not much interested in housework. As for my story, there's not much to tell."

"Oh, dear. There's always something to tell, questions and ideas and dreams floating around in a young woman's head. And nobody gets through the growing-up years without their share of hurts. Tell me and I'll listen."

I don't know whether Abby cast a spell over me with her sad eyes or whether I was taken aback at having someone ask me what was going on inside my head, but before I knew it my thoughts started spilling out. I told her about the trouble with Mama and about how lonely I was going to be if I didn't have Jimmy to talk to. I even told her about how I hated my new body and how I didn't understand why growing up had to be so hard. She listened, not once looking away. I told her things I didn't even know I'd been thinking. When I finished, I felt clean inside, like I'd thrown out a dishpan of greasy water, rinsed it, and watched the last drops sparkle in the sunlight.

We lay back on our bed of grass, and as I watched fleecy clouds pass overhead, a line from that Bible verse drifted into my head. *A time to speak and a time to be silent.*

After a while, the old woman said, "It's time for me to be moving on."

"Where will you go?"

"To a beautiful place like this meadow here, where a body's never hungry or cold."

"Take me with you. Oh, please take me with you." A world of imagined adventure unfolded before my eyes.

"Oh, no, Anna, it's no place for you. You belong here with your family, here on this land. You've got spunk. I can tell. You'll make something of yourself one day, mark my words. But I would like to give you a little gift before I go."

She tugged a thin gold band from the ring finger of her right hand. "This was my mother's ring, and her mother's before her."

"Oh, no, I couldn't."

"I want you to have it. All I ask is that one day you pass the ring on to another young woman, and with the giving of the gift that you tell the story of how Mother and I once passed this way."

She slipped the ring on my finger. It was a perfect fit.

"But I have no gift to give to you," I said, admiring the way the gold glittered in the sunlight.

"First fetch an old woman a cool drink; then, when you return, you'll know the one precious gift you can give me."

Not wanting to tangle with the barbed wire, I took the long way home. To compensate, I ran all the way. When I reached the end of our lane, I ducked behind the row of lilac bushes and emptied pebbles from my shoes while I checked out the farmyard to see if my path was clear. Parked in the yard was Ramona's black De Soto. I wondered how Mama had accounted for my absence. She'd most likely told the ladies that I'd gone off with Daddy.

I tiptoed through the garden Mama had planted around the base of the windmill, the only place she could keep her vegetables watered and alive. The air should have been filled with sounds — blades groaning, water gurgling up and into the pipe. I licked my index finger and raised it above my head. The breeze I'd felt minutes before in the meadow had died. I followed the pipe the few feet to its end. Only a few drops fell, plink, plunk, into the round stock tank. After grabbing the handle of the oak bucket, I swooped it into the tank. If it had been Mama I was fetching the drink for, she would have gasped, saying, "Drinking after the cows." But I drank from it often, scooping up water with my hands. I swam there too, and I hadn't yet come down with hoof-and-mouth disease.

The water lapped over the brim of my bucket as I hurried toward the spot where we'd had our little chat. When I reached that place, the only sign of Abby was the impression her body had made in the grass. Two cabbage butterflies, who had been resting nearby, spread their wings and fluttered across the meadow. I followed. It seemed the thing to do. I hadn't gone more than twenty paces when the handle of Daddy's shovel caught my eye. A little farther along, I saw that the shovel was stuck in a pile of dirt — freshly dug dirt, but dry on the surface, as if it had been dug a day or two before. I crawled to the peak of the pile, moved a very heavy canvas rucksack aside, and peered over the edge into a deep hole. One of

Daddy's ladders leaned against the side of the hole, and at the bottom lay a quilt done up in a log cabin pattern. The quilt was lumpy, like the one on my bed, but lumpy in the shape of a woman.

"Come on out of there. You'll catch your death of cold," I shouted. There was no answer or movement. I waited a bit, then called again. Still nothing. "Okay, I'm coming down after you."

I was good at ladders, so getting down was easy. The problem was where to stand when I reached the bottom. The hole was only wide and long enough for one body. I straddled the lump, careful not to step on any parts of it, and slowly folded back the quilt. Abby's hair, freed from its bun, flowed like honey over her shoulders. A bouquet of prairie roses blossomed from her prayerful hands. And she was wearing Jane's blue dress! She looked peaceful, the way babies look when, tummies full, they nod off to sleep. But there was something in her wide-open, unblinking eyes that hadn't been there before. They weren't sad anymore. *Unblinking?*

I jiggled her shoulder, but there was no response, so I grabbed a hunk of arm skin and pinched hard. Nothing. One hand holding the ladder for balance, I leaned over to listen for breathing sounds. The ladder shifted and I fell, ending up eyeball to eyeball with Abby. I scrambled to my feet, managing to step on one of her bosoms in the process. When she didn't cry out at that, not a crumb of doubt remained. Abby was dead.

Why? How? She'd been talking to me a short time before. And she must have been strong to have traveled all the way from Ohio and to dig such a deep hole. She'd said she would be moving on, on to a better place, "a beautiful place like this meadow here, where a body's never hungry or cold." *Heaven?* Yes, she'd come back to our meadow to die.

Before I climbed up the ladder, I rearranged the crushed prairie roses and smoothed the quilt, being extra careful to pat out all but the womanly lumps.

The air above seemed almost too hot and heavy to breathe. With my heart beating as fast as hummingbird wings, I sat down atop the mound. "Why me?" I asked, looking up at the sky. About then, a clod of dirt tumbled over the edge, carrying other clods with it. Abby's words came back to me. "You'll know the one precious gift you can give me."

I pulled up the ladder, then inched my way to the shovel. With my fingers wrapped in a tight grip about the handle, I thrust the blade into the dirt pile, swung it over the hole, and tipped it. Pebbles sprinkled down, sounding like raindrops pattering on thirsty earth.

* * *

When the mound of dirt over the grave was packed as tightly as I could pack it, when I had hidden the mound with fistfuls of uprooted grass, and when my shirt was soaked through with perspiration, the sun was noon high in the sky.

There was one more thing that needed to be done. A proper burying required godly words. *A preacher? No.* I knew I couldn't tell anybody, or they'd dig her up and plant her in the cemetery in town. She hadn't come all that way to be put to rest next to a bunch of strangers. This would be my secret, until it was time for me to pass on Abby's story and her ring to another young woman, a far piece down the road. I'd shoveled my way right into a mysterious past.

I wished then that I'd paid more attention in Sunday School. I folded my hands and prayed the Lord's Prayer — the only prayer I knew by heart. It didn't seem enough, though, so I strung together more pieces of the verse. *A time to laugh, a time to dance, a time to love, a time of peace.*

I said a couple of amens, then sat down and opened Abby's rucksack. Inside I found the old clothes she'd been wearing, a beaded pouch filled with a rainbow of colored stones, a bundle of yellowing letters, and a dirt-crusted Mason jar filled to the brim with gold coins! She had found Helmer's gold. Enough gold to buy back some of Mama and Daddy's lost happiness. Enough gold to buy my way into our Model-T Ford come

Saturday night. I wanted to run back to the house right then, and give the coins to Mama, but my bones were too tired.

I lay down atop Abby's grave and let sleep have its way with me. And while I slept, I dreamed that I was a grown woman sitting among the wildflowers in the meadow. Golden butterflies fluttered nearby. A baby, swaddled in pink, cooed as she nuzzled my breast.

The dream shattered with Mama's distant call.

"A-n-n-a. Show yourself this instant."

Seven

By the time Anna had finished telling her story, the baby calf, its belly full of first milk, had curled up next to its mother and fallen asleep. Anna, her own eyes drooping, yawned and said, "I've finally run out of words. I think it's time I put my old bones to bed."

I wanted to ask her questions, especially about Jimmy, but tucked them away for another time. I did walk back to the house with Anna, but I didn't go to bed. I retrieved a large sketchpad and returned to the barn, where I sketched several pictures of the calf before curling up on the straw sofa and falling asleep.

I awoke to loud mooing, from cow 712 in the next stall. After rubbing the sleep from my eyes, I slowly rolled off the straw sofa and peeked over the stall wall. Cow 712 mooed again, and with the second moo, delivered her baby calf into the straw. Like before, the calf didn't move, didn't breathe. I waited for the cow to lick life into her baby, waited as she awkwardly stood, one sharp hoof just missing the calf's still body, waited as she moved as far away from her calf as her rope lead allowed. My heart pounding in my ears, I dashed around the stall wall. "Your baby needs you," I shouted, tugging at 712's halter. She didn't budge an inch. "What kind of a mother are you?" I screamed, digging in my heels and leaning my shoulder hard into her flank. She swished her tail as if I were nothing more than a pesky fly.

What happened next probably took only a few seconds, but it felt like a lifetime. I rinsed my trembling hands in the water bucket, then knelt beside the motionless calf. "Breathe, breathe like this," I shouted, gulping air in and out, in and out. Nothing, not a twitch, so I grabbed handfuls of straw and used them like tongues to lick life into the calf. I'd just begun to imagine how I might perform CPR on a calf, how I might blow my own air into its mouth, how to know where on its chest to place my hands so I could jump-start its brand new heart, when the calf sucked in one startled breath, and then a second. Its chest rose and fell, rose and fell again. A round eye opened. A hind leg stretched, but I didn't stop wiping until the shivering calf was nearly dry, didn't stop wiping until my own tear-dampened cheeks were nearly dry.

Cow 712 mooed, and I looked up. She stomped and reared her head back so hard I thought her lead would snap. She stomped again. "No way," I said, sliding my arms under the calf. The calf weighed more than I'd expected, more than Anna's water-filled galvanized bucket, but Anna wasn't there to offer a hand, so I reached inside myself, found strength I didn't know I had, and carried the calf to the straw sofa, safely out of 712's stomping reach. The calf was gaining wiggly strength, too, and I was afraid she'd roll off the sofa and hurt herself. I pinned her down with one hand while I tore chunks of straw from the edges of the bales. The more I tore, the more the center of the sofa loosened and sagged, finally settling into a soft, floor-level bed.

The calf was still shivering, so I lay down and cradled her to my body like we were two spoons. New tears tumbled down my cheeks, joyful tears this time. I'd held babies before, marveled at the softness of their skin and the miniature size of their hands, but this was different. This calf, a life that hadn't existed a few minutes before, a life so simple and right, this straw-covered calf, was mine. Not mine in the sense that I owned her, but mine in my heart. She deserved more than a number. She deserved a name. I named her Straw, then like a thunderbolt, I remembered what Anna had said about calves needing first milk. I unspooned myself from Straw and raced for the house.

*   *   *

I'd just reached the back porch steps when I heard Sarah and Anna talking in the kitchen. There was something in their tone that made me stop.

"Have you taken leave of your senses?" Anna said. "I'd never intentionally come between you and Hope."

"How do you explain the fact that the two of you spent half the night in the barn, that you didn't bother to wake me? I'd wanted this summer to be perfect, planned it all out, but now I'm beginning to think bringing her here was a bad idea."

"A bad idea for her or for you?" Anna calmly asked.

"What do you mean?"

"Think about it," Anna answered.

Part of me wanted to walk away, to pretend that I hadn't heard what I'd just heard, but the calf needed its mother's first milk. For that I needed Anna.

"I need help," I said rushing in.

Sarah's cheeks reddened.

"What is it?" Anna asked.

"There's a second calf, and the mother won't take care of it."

The three of us spent most of the morning in the barn. Once Straw had learned to use her legs,

Anna nudged her toward 712's udder. The cow kicked, barely missing Straw's head.

Though Anna coaxed and even threatened a swift kick of her own, 712 continued to refuse her baby. Anna finally gave up and milked 712 by hand. Her fingers moved rhythmically up and down, two teats at a time, the milk squirting into a special bucket that had a rubber nipple attached to the bottom. When Anna had milked 712 dry, she handed the bucket to me. "I think you should have the honor of the first feeding."

At first, much of the milk dribbled down Straw's chin, but it didn't take her long to get the butt and pull of it. By the time the bucket was empty, her belly bulged.

Later, after Straw had gotten good at using her legs, Anna introduced her to cow 568. "How would you like two babies?" Anna asked. Cow 568 sniffed Straw, sniffed her own calf, swished her tail, then resumed chewing her cud.

I might have stayed in the barn the rest of the day if I hadn't needed a shower so badly, and I might have stayed in the shower the rest of the day if the hot water hadn't run out, and I might have stayed in Sarah's old room, drawing sketches of Straw, if the aroma of Sarah's chicken soup hadn't made my stomach growl.

In the kitchen, Sarah had set the table with two blue-specked bowls.

"Where's Anna?" I asked.

"When she heard on the radio that it's supposed to rain all afternoon, she decided to visit her sister at the nursing home," Sarah answered, spooning soup into my bowl.

"Nursing home?"

Sarah pulled out a chair and sat down. "Mom hates that Jane has to be there. She took care of her here at home for as long as she could, longer than she should have, in fact. Aunt Jane was never an easy woman to be around, and Alzheimer's has only made it worse. Mom's faithful, though, visits her at least once a week. Usually, she takes this shoebox of pictures with her, hoping that one of the photos will trigger Jane's memory, but today she left in such a hurry she must have forgotten."

Sarah spread a handful of photographs across the table. One of them accidentally drifted to the floor. I picked it up. In it a teenage boy, dressed in farmer's overalls, was straddling Anna's Cushman scooter.

"Is this Jimmy?"

Sarah leaned forward. "No, that's not my dad, that's my uncle Henry, and that's the Cushman when it was new. When Mom came home from the meadow the day she buried Abigail, toting the jar of Helmer's gold, Grandpa Otto gave one coin each to Mom, Jane, and Henry, and he told them they could spend it any way they wished. Henry spent his twenty-dollar Liberty Double Eagle on the scooter."

"What wish did Anna buy?"

"Mom said that bringing home the gold was wish enough for her. The money in that jar paid off the back taxes, which saved the farm. Mom still has her Double Eagle around here somewhere. The last time she checked it was worth about eight hundred dollars."

"What does Henry look like now?" I asked, imagining age lines on his handsome young face.

"I'm sorry to say that Henry lost his life in World War II."

Sarah slid another photo across the table. "This is Jane on her wedding day. She used her gold coin to buy the dress."

Thunder, which had been rumbling in the distance since we'd come in from the barn, boomed so loudly the windows rattled.

"Did she marry that Bucky guy?"

"Unfortunately, yes. Mom says Grandma Rebecca tried to talk her out of marrying Buck, but Jane was convinced he was the only person who could make her happy."

"Did he make her happy?"

Lightning flashed, and the kitchen light flickered.

"Buck had his good points, but he wasn't much of a husband — or farmer. He overworked his land and let his machinery sit out rusting in all kinds of weather. Eventually he lost his farm to bad debt."

The phone rang. "Here's one you'll be interested in," Sarah said, getting up. "This is Grandma Rebecca and Grandpa Otto, taken not long after their wedding day."

I didn't pay attention to what Sarah was saying into the phone because I was studying Rebecca's face. The sketch I had drawn of her was different, but not that different. Her hair was dark, her jaw had the same square shape, and the mystery was there, in her eyes. Standing beside her was Otto, looking proud.

"That was Mom," Sarah said, hurrying back to the table. "I don't want to frighten you, but she says the sirens are going off in town, and that the Weather Service has issued a tornado warning."

"Will she be okay?" I asked, shooting a glance out the window. The sky was gray-green, and rain was coming down in sheets.

"She'll be fine. They're moving all the residents into the interior hallways. It's us she's worried about. Someone's spotted a funnel cloud five miles west of here, so we need to take shelter in the cave."

"Cave?"

"Lots of farms have them in their yards, especially the ones that don't have cellars under the house, like this one."

We were on the back porch when the wind hit, alarming Rebecca's dinner bell — clang, clang, clang. Sarah plucked two hooded rain slickers from their nails and handed one to me. I put mine on over my backpack, then followed Sarah down the steps and across the yard. The cave, which on the surface resembled a grass-covered turtle shell, squatted a few feet from the gravel driveway. A wooden door slanted up at one end, and Sarah was having trouble lifting it.

"Let me help," I shouted over the hiss of the wind; then I placed my hand next to hers on the curved, rust-crusted handle.

"On the count of three," Sarah shouted back. "One, two, lift." The door opened like a slow yawn, but there was nothing slow about the earthy odor that rushed up the narrow steps, and nothing slow about the way we and three of Anna's drenched cats scrambled down.

In the dark at the bottom, Sarah said, "How stupid of me. I should have brought a kerosene lantern. Stay here. I'll go back up and get one."

"Wait," I said, sliding one arm out of the slicker so I could get at my backpack. Using my fingers as eyes, I found the familiar shape of my flashlight, drew it out, flicked it on, and handed it to Sarah.

Sarah immediately aimed the flashlight at the

cave's arched brick ceiling. "We'll be safe down here, snug as a bug in a rug," she said, but the quiver in her voice gave her away.

"Are you okay?" I asked.

"I'm fine. It's just that I get a little claustrophobic in small, enclosed spaces."

She then turned the flashlight on me. "Are you frightened?"

"I'm fine," I answered. What Sarah didn't know was that I'd been caught in bad storms before, not tornadoes, but storms with wind angry enough to topple giant trees. I'd taken shelter where I'd found it, glass bus-stop enclosures, twenty-four-hour convenience stores, strangers' garages, and once even a vacant dog house. I'd always been alone, so the cave felt almost comfy.

"We can go back up if you want," I said.

"Absolutely not. It's my responsibility to keep you safe. I'll be fine if I keep my mind busy, so why don't we see what treasures Mom has stored down here."

As Sarah shone her flashlight across a row of wooden shelves, I wondered about the idea of safety. Could one person give it, like a gift, to another?

Hailstones clattered against the cave door. Sarah flinched, then said, "Look at the label on this jar of peaches. It's dated August 1958. This must be a jar Grandma Rebecca and I put up the summer before she died."

"Would it be safe to eat?"

"Could be. I don't see any mold or discoloration, but that's no guarantee that it's safe. I'm sure Mom kept it all these years because it was something of Grandma Rebecca's."

"Is canning hard to do?"

"Not if you have a teacher like Grandma Rebecca. After Grandpa Otto died in 1957, Mom took over all the farm work, which meant she had to spend a lot of time in the fields and barn. Grandma Rebecca, as she was fond of saying, took me under her wing. She patiently taught me the art of homemaking. I loved it, all of it. The musical plink-plink of canning lids sealing in unison, the aroma of bread rising in the oven, the hypnotic rhythm of the sewing-machine treadle, the sheen of a freshly waxed floor. I just wish she'd lived longer, so I could have learned even more."

"When did Rebecca die?"

"It was the winter I was eleven, and Grandma Rebecca was having a hard time getting over a bout with the flu. Though she kept saying that she didn't want to cause a fuss, Mom finally convinced her to see old Doc Drucker. He discovered a walnut-sized lump in her right breast and another lump under her arm. When Doc asked Grandma Rebecca how it was that she hadn't felt the lumps, Mom said she had blushed and said she was raised to believe that it was a sin to touch her body with anything but a washcloth. Isn't that sad? Hope, if you ever have any questions about your body, any questions, please ask. And if you feel more comfortable asking Mom, I'm okay with that too."

I wasn't sure what to say, so I said, "Okay."

"Good, because not asking can have devastating consequences, like it did for Grandma Rebecca. Her cancer had gone undetected too long and had spread beyond the point of treatment. Near the end, Mom put a bed in the parlor, and we took turns sitting by her side. Her thoughts slipped back in time. She'd ask when Henry was coming in from the field or try to get out of bed, sure that Otto was in the next room, sick with the fever. But in her last hours, it was her mum that she called out for. Rebecca's last words were a question. 'Did I make Papa proud?' 'Button-popping proud,' Mom answered just before Rebecca slipped away."

I turned away from Sarah then, into the dark, to hide a sudden burst of tears. Sarah placed her hand on my shoulder. I didn't shrug it away, didn't move until a lightning bolt split the air with a deafening crack. Sarah and I both jumped, as did one of Anna's cats, who leaped down from the shelf, where it had been snoozing.

"I can't believe these are still here," Sarah said, reaching for some paper booklets the cat had been using as a lap.

"What are they?" I asked, glad for the distraction.

"This one's a civil defense brochure, published in 1960."

"How did it get down here in the cave?"

"I suppose I left it here. They handed these awful things out at school, to twelve-year-olds, no less. In here are step-by-step instructions for building a fallout shelter."

"A fallout shelter?"

"Yes, a fallout shelter. The government said it was everyone's patriotic duty to build one. It's laughable now, like they believed all-out nuclear war was survivable, but I wasn't laughing then. I was scared silly. It was the time of the Cold War, and B52 bombers, from the Strategic Air Command in Omaha, flew practice runs over our farm. I was terrified that one of those wide-winged silver hawks would accidentally lay its annihilation egg smack in the middle of our hen house.

"And school, a place I'd always thought of as next to heaven, became a house of horrors. One *Weekly Reader* had a story about the Atlas missile the air force was testing, which was capable of carrying its payload up to nine thousand miles. I remember hunching over the world atlas, calculating the distance between Omaha and Moscow. If we had a missile that flew that far, it was a safe bet the Soviets had one too. And then there were the air-raid drills. When the sirens blared, we crouched under our desks, hands clamped like nutcrackers over our heads. After one of these drills, I approached Mrs. MacKnight, my sixth-grade teacher, and told her I couldn't hear the sirens on the farm. She told me not to worry, that I'd know when to duck for cover when I saw the bomb's brilliant white lig — "

The loudest crack of thunder yet stopped Sarah midword. She dropped the brochure and grabbed my hand.

"Keep talking," I said, lacing my fingers with hers.

"Talk. Right. I'll just keep talking. The brochures. The brochures they handed out, handed out at school — I studied them until I knew the fallout shelter plans by heart: the dimensions of the concrete walls, the thickness of the steel doors, the mechanics of the air-filtration system. Wanting one in the worst way, I worked on Mom for about a week. I tucked one brochure under the knife next to her plate and another inside her underwear drawer. But it was the one I baked into the jelly roll that got her attention. She rinsed her mouth out, then smiled and said we'd have to build ours the size of Noah's ark, else who would tend to the livestock?

"That's when I came up with the idea of using this cave as a shelter. I stocked it with canned goods and gallon jugs of water, army cots and candles, a wind-up clock and calendar. Air filtration was a problem I never solved, and I think I knew that the tin foil I'd taped to the inside of the door wouldn't stop the radiation, but there were the bricks, the six feet of solid earth overhead."

Sarah looked up again, and her hand began to tremble. I squeezed it gently and asked, "What did Anna think of your fallout shelter?"

Sarah squeezed back. "She probably thought I'd gone nuts, but of course she didn't say that. She praised me for being so clever and industrious. She also encouraged me to talk about my fears, which I did endlessly. I also wrote about those times, though not until three years later, when I was a sophomore in high school. If this storm ever goes away, I'd like to share my story with you."

I was wishing hard for the storm to go away, quick, when a sound erupted — not thunder, but more like a continuous elephant's trumpet, distant at first, then closer. Closer. Sarah and I turned toward one another. Her eyes reflected my question; my eyes reflected hers. Closer still, and the cave began to shudder. As if thinking we could hold up the earth if it began to fall, we unclasped our hands and braced them against the arched brick ceiling. Then came a moment of quiet, followed by a metallic thud. More quiet. The cave door was lifting up. A blinding burst of gray light entered. A voice. "Anna, are you down there?"

Sarah nudged me toward the bottom step. "Is that you, Lloyd?" Sarah called back.

"Last time I looked in the mirror it was," he answered back.

"What a relief. We thought you were the tornado. What's it like up there?"

"Still raining, but the worst part of the storm has passed to the east, so it's safe for you to come on out of there."

"Thank God," Sarah said to me as we climbed the cave steps. "If you hadn't been down there with me, been so calm, I would have lost it for sure."

Though I hadn't done anything special, I felt an unfamiliar tickle of pride.

In the aboveground world again, Sarah drew in several deep breaths, then turned to Lloyd Stuhr and asked, "What was that awful noise we heard before you opened the cave door?"

"Sorry about that. I started laying on my truck horn as soon as I turned in the lane. It's a signal Anna and I have worked out. Saves time in an emergency."

"An emergency?"

"I heard on my scanner that the tornado touched down between here and Prairie Hill. The reports are still sketchy, but there's been at least one call for an ambulance. I'm headed over there to see if I can help, and I figured Anna would want to go with me. She's the first person folks ask for when trouble knocks on their door."

"Mom's in town today," Sarah said, and then

she began chewing her bottom lip the way she always does when there is a problem to be solved. When she stopped chewing she said, "Maybe Hope and I could follow you in my car, see if there's anything we could do to help."

"I wouldn't recommend it," Lloyd said. "Could be trees across the road, power lines down. If you want to go, you should ride with me. My truck's built like a tank, but I'm afraid I can only squeeze one more in my cab. I've brought my son, Jake, along."

I peeked at Lloyd's truck. A grinning teenage boy, wearing a Nebraska Cornhuskers sports cap, peeked back.

"Go," I said, turning to Sarah.

"No, I should stay here with you."

"I'll be fine. Go and see if there's anything you can do to help."

"Are you sure?"

"I'm sure."

"How long do you think we'll be gone?" Sarah asked Lloyd.

"Hard to say; it could be an hour, could be four. Depends on how much damage has been done. There could be livestock to corral, broken windows or damaged roofs to board up." Lloyd looked at his watch. "If you're coming, we'd better get a move on."

"She's coming," I said.

"Okay, you've twisted my arm, but you have to promise me you'll stay close to the house."

"I promise. Now go."

Before they drove away, Sarah leaned out the truck window and said, "Give Anna a call, tell her we're okay. The number for the nursing home is by the phone."

"Be careful," I said, waving, then went straight to the barn to make sure Straw had come through the storm okay. She was fine, prancing around the stall as if she'd been using her legs for weeks, not hours.

Back at the house, the kitchen light didn't come on when I flipped the switch, and when I picked up the phone to call Anna, the line was dead. The only thing that worked was the grandfather clock, which chimed twice.

I sat in the same chair I'd sat in at lunch, the same chair I'd sat in at every meal since I'd arrived, and pulled a small sketchpad from my backpack. The sketch I drew of the cave was a cutaway, half above ground, half below. The sky swirled, and the cave, surrounded by solid, penciled-in earth, arched with light. In the arch stood one, then two, then five hooded figures, their arms raised as if holding up the earth.

I'd just signed my name to the sketch when the clock chimed once, meaning only a half-hour had passed. I was used to finding ways of filling up empty time — digging, searching. But that day I had no interest in digging, and I was too far from Minneapolis to search, so I decided to fill the time with work. Chores. I began by spooning the left-over soup from the kettle into a Tupperware bowl, burping the lid like I'd seen Sarah do, and I slid the bowl into the darkened refrigerator. After that, I found a straw broom and swept my way from the kitchen into the dining room, into the front hall, and out the door, where I swept soggy leaves off the front veranda. Then, leaning on my broom as Rebecca had once done, I admired the rows of shaggy cedar trees Abby had planted.

In Anna's room, I patted out the lumps in her box-of-sixty-four crayon-colored quilt. In Sarah's old room, I turned this way and that in front of the vanity mirror, studying my not-curvaceous-but-okay reflection, then gathered my dirty clothes into a neat pile and wondered if Anna kept an old-fashioned scrub board around anywhere. In the room Sarah had been using, Otto's old room, Henry's maybe, I found no chores to do. The only thing that looked out of place was a red three-ring notebook that lay in the center of . . . ? Could it be? Yes, it was Minna's quilt, the one Rebecca had described in her journal, the one with a girl dangling her bare feet into the tree-lined brook. I was about to move the notebook aside so I could see the quilted scene as a whole when I noticed the notebook's label: "My Story,

November 1963." I drew my hand away as if from a hot stove.

This must be the story Sarah had said she wanted to share with me. I was staring at it, wondering if I dared read it, when a drop of water detonated on the label. I looked up just as another drop fell from the gold gizmo at the tip of the light fixture. I picked the notebook up, wiped away the water with my hand, and laid it down again on the pillow. A third drop fell, landing on the quilt-girl's cheek.

I wasn't anxious to go up into the attic, remembering what Anna had said about ghosts, but I knew I couldn't wait until Sarah or Anna came home to fix the problem. Water and electricity didn't mix, a lesson I'd learned from my mother when I'd stood tippy-toes on a chair at the kitchen counter in one of the apartments we'd lived in and pulled the toaster too close to the water-filled sink. It was the only time I remember her yelling at me. So what if the electricity came back on? A short, a spark, a fire, and the house and all its memories could turn to ash. I couldn't let that happen.

The attic stairs were narrow and steep, like the ones in the cave; only they led up, not down. I let my feet fall hard on each tread as a way of announcing my arrival, just in case. At the top, I kept my eyes out of the darkest shadows and focused on finding the source of the drips. I sketched a map of the second floor on the paper of my imagination and headed for the spot I thought was above Sarah's bed. A wall of boxes stopped me, but I heard a drip, so I began moving the heavy boxes aside. When I'd cleared away two stacks, I found a metal bucket, just out of the puddle's reach. I slid the bucket under the roof drip — plink, plunk — then ran down two flights of stairs to get a mop.

I also grabbed a bath towel and my flashlight on my way back up. After dabbing the quilt-girl's cheek, I spread the towel over her face to protect her from what had quickly become a waterfall of new drips, then dashed up the attic steps. Anna's mop wasn't like the squeeze-sponge mops most of my foster moms had used. Clumped on its head were long, thick cords, like clowns' hair, which drank up the puddle with only a couple of swirls. Then I stood back, aimed the flashlight beam at the rafters, and made a game of guessing when the next drip would drop, plink, into the bucket. In time, the drips grew further apart, which was good but boring, so I decided to explore.

At the far end of the attic, beneath the small window Rebecca had described in her journal, I found her metal cot. It had no mattress, only a web of wire, which pricked my back when I lay down briefly. Beside the cot stood a small painted chest. Neatly folded in the drawer was a badly faded and frayed blue dress, Eva's dress, Rebecca's dress, I was sure. I held the dress up to my shoulders, turning this way and that, and knew without trying the dress on that it would fit me perfectly.

The floor creaked. Once. Twice. I turned around to see a blurry figure dressed in blue. Two hands flew to two mouths. Two blue dresses fell to the floor. Two figures stepped back. One step. Two. Then cautiously, carefully, forward three. Two hands brushed a circle of dust from the face in a standup mirror. One inside, one out, like a mime. My thoughts spun, like a gerbil on a wheel. Were we one, or were we two? If two, then which one was real? The one inside the mirror or the one outside? And then the gerbil stopped. I was the impostor, the one who'd been making believe, like a little girl clomping around in her mother's shoes. Sweeping the veranda like Rebecca, patting out lumps like Anna. Belonging wasn't a dress I could simply slip over my head. I picked up Eva's dress from the floor, smoothed out any wrinkles I may have made, and returned it to its rightful place in the drawer before heading down the attic steps.

At the kitchen table again, I deliberately sat in a different chair from the one I'd sat in before and erased the fifth, what-had-I-been-thinking, figure I'd drawn inside the cave, then began digging through Anna's picture box. I was looking for the oldest pictures, the ones that were more beige and brown than black and white. Though I did find a couple of young women I couldn't name, I knew in my heart that none of them were Eva, so I sketched her. Above the churning creek waters, I strung a footbridge for her to cross safely. And in case the bridge might fall, I gave her sturdy wings.

After that, I pulled out a color photo of Sarah, one with the words "School Days, 1963–64" printed at the bottom. She was wearing a white blouse with small blue flowers embroidered on each side of a rounded collar. Her hair shone in the photographer's light and flipped up so perfectly at the shoulders I guessed that she'd set it with curlers. The corners of her mouth smiled, but her eyes didn't. Her eyes were worried. I was wondering what it was she was worrying about in 1963, when the dates clicked, like a key opening a lock. The notebook on Sarah's bed was dated 1963, and the answer was lying there on her bed. The question was, Should I read it?

I wrestled with that question for the rest of the afternoon and into the evening, through the dozen or so times I picked up the phone to see if it was working, through four noisy trips to the attic to make sure the bucket hadn't moved, on its own or otherwise. I wrestled through three coats of nail polish and through the first pages of nearly every book on Anna's bookshelf, through a peanut-butter-and-pickle sandwich, which I washed down with two glasses of quickly warming milk. I wrestled through countless trips to the barn, wrestled with a growing and new kind of worry. Why hadn't Sarah or Anna returned? Were they safe, or had something bad happened to one or both of them?

My wrestling ended when it got dark. Dark on a farm without electricity is really, really dark. No passing headlights bending through the windows, no glowing emergency exit signs, just black. And oh so silent. Only the in and out of my breath and bursts of thoughts ricocheting inside my head.

Worried that my flashlight batteries might soon grow weak, I retrieved four wooden matches from a metal container that hung on the wall near Anna's stove. I broke three matches before I managed to light a large white candle I'd found in the parlor. The scent of vanilla followed me up the flickery stairs and down the hall into Sarah's room, where I placed the candle on the nightstand. I sat on the bed, my back propped against the pillow, and opened the notebook to the sound of Sarah's typewritten young voice.

Eight

November 27, 1963

Five days ago, on November 22, 1963, a few minutes before the bell that would signal the end of the lunch period, I was sitting in the school library, working off the last hour of a five-hour detention. I'd been given the detention for putting words in the mouth of the George Washington statue that stands at the end of the main hall. I'd protested, because George hadn't been harmed in any way. The cardboard word balloon, which read "Ban Nuclear Testing," had been attached with an elastic loop that I'd carefully slipped over his marble head.

As always, I was putting the detention time to good use by working on a report for my American government class. The assignment, which wasn't due for a week, was to write four or five pages about President Kennedy's first thousand days in office. I'd already written nine. My title, "Rejoicing in Hope, Patient in Tribulation," was a quote from President Kennedy's inaugural address. I'd

164

chosen this title because it perfectly summarized what I wanted to say — "hope" that JFK would continue to make the world a kinder and safer place to live, and "patient" because JFK's work wasn't finished.

I'd written a paragraph each on his plans to build new schools, to provide better housing for the poor, and to guarantee affordable health care for the elderly. I'd written a full page on the Peace Corps, two on the treaty that had banned above-ground nuclear testing, and four about JFK's success at ridding Cuba of Soviet missiles. I might have written even more on the missile crisis in Cuba, about how close we'd come to nuclear war, if I hadn't kept remembering what it had felt like to think I was going to die. I'd written that nuclear testing was still happening, underground in the Nevada desert, and about rumors of American troops being sent to South Vietnam, a country I'd had to look up in a world atlas to find.

That day in the school library, I was adding another inaugural quote to my report — "All this will not be finished in the first hundred days. Nor will it be finished in the first thousand days" — when my best friend, Allison, slid into the chair next to mine.

"Have you heard?" she whispered.

I thought she was asking if I'd heard that Lloyd Stuhr had invited Julie Jacobsen to the Future Farmers of America Harvest Ball.

165

"Julie told me, and I think it's really neat."

Allison looked at me as if I'd (a) just stepped out of *Twilight Zone,* (b) joined the Communist Party, or (c) gotten something less than an A on my report card.

"You were asking if I'd heard about Julie and Lloyd, right?"

"No, it's not that. I just heard that . . . that President Kennedy has been shot."

An imagined bullet slammed into my chest. "He's still alive, right?"

Allison nodded, then pulled her transistor radio from her purse and handed it to me under the table. Ordinarily I would have looked up to see if Mrs. Dierking, the librarian, had her antenna pointed our way, but this wasn't ordinary.

Soon a crowd had gathered around us, including Mrs. Dierking, who asked me to turn the volume up. It was as if Allison's radio were a magnet holding our eyes and our breath, pulling more students in from the hall. Except for the somber radio voices and the occasional squeak of a shoe on the polished wooden floor, the room was as silent as a prayer — a prayer that ended with the explosive amen of the fifth-hour warning bell, startling me so much I almost ducked for cover under the table.

When the tardy bell rang, no one moved, and I don't think we would have moved if Mr. Baxter, the principal, hadn't come in and told us we had to go to class.

I left the library with the rest, but I didn't go to my Advanced English 10 class. I walked down the hall, out the door, and slid behind the wheel of my Studebaker, which was older than me and as beat up as I felt. I'd paid $35 for the car, money I'd earned from a summer's worth of corn detasseling. I'd named the car Hope for "hope she gets me there, hope she gets me home." Sooner or later, she usually did. But that day, Hope got me only halfway home to our second-hand Zenith TV before she began to sputter. I managed to coax her to the shoulder before she died.

I knew she'd spark back to life again if I gave her the time she needed to cool off, but I didn't know where I'd find the patience. President Kennedy was lying in a hospital bed in Dallas, dying maybe, maybe already dead, and there I sat, in a car without a radio, on a rarely traveled country road. "He will be okay. He will," I said to myself as if believing could make it so.

I spent the next thirty minutes adding to my report, but I didn't write about JFK's first thousand days. I wrote about his next next thousand, imagining a safe future for him in headlines. Among these were: November 23, 1963: "JFK Expected to Recover"; November 30,1963: "JFK Released from Dallas Hospital"; March 14, 1964:

"JFK Signs Nuclear Test Ban Treaty"; November 7, 1964: "Kennedy Defeats Nixon, Again"; July 10, 1965: "Jackie Gives Birth to Healthy Baby Boy"; April 16, 1966: "JFK Negotiates Peace in Vietnam"; October 12, 1966: "World Powers Sign Nuclear Disarmament Agreement"; September 5, 1967: "Last Atlas Missile Silo Dismantled."

I ended my list with January 1, 2000: "JFK Dies Peacefully in His Sleep." Then I pressed Hope's clutch to the floor. "I believe you are ready to go home," I said and turned the key in the ignition. She started on the first try, and we went home. Home to learn the awful truth.

I turned in my report today, unchanged from the way it was the day President Kennedy died. I expect I will get an A, but I wish now that I'd written a different report, one about why I wrote such a long report in the first place, or as I learned in English class, "the story behind the story." I've tried to write this story before, but I wanted the writing to be perfect. It never was. This time I have given myself permission not to be perfect. And my mom has given me an idea I think will help. She has suggested that I write my story as if I were telling it to a daughter I might one day have.

So, dear future daughter, this is for you.

My story begins in late June 1960, when I was
thirteen. I was preparing lunch and had gone
down into the cave, which was also my makeshift
fallout shelter, to get a jar of canned peaches,
when I heard the rumble of a car driving up our
lane. Brutus heard it too and barked up a storm. I
thought it was the Fuller Brush salesman. He was
the only person Brutus ever got worked up about,
but when I climbed the cave steps, I saw it wasn't
the Fuller Brush man that Brutus's front paws
had pinned to the door of a black sedan.

"Down, Brutus. Down!" I shouted.

Brutus, his tongue lolling out the side of his
mouth, looked at me in a way that said, "Oh
please let me eat this man's face. Oh please."

"Don't you even think it." I jerked him down
by the collar.

The man brushed the dusty paw prints off his
double-breasted jacket and adjusted the knot in
his narrow tie. "You ought to keep that dog
chained up."

"He's as harmless as a marshmallow, most of
the time."

"I'm here to see Anna Foster. Is she home?"

He had this dreamy voice, like Dick Clark on
American Bandstand. "No, she's taken Ferdinand, her prize-winning Hereford bull, over to

one of the neighbors, to, you know, service his cows, but she'll be back in a few minutes." I couldn't take my eyes off him. And he was there to see Mom. I shifted my ogle to his ring finger. Bare.

"You're welcome to come inside and wait."

He shot a look at Brutus, who was straining at his collar. "Wouldn't mind if I do."

As we stepped into the kitchen, I tried to see it through a stranger's eyes. We had no wall of matching aquamarine cupboards, no automatic Maytag washer, no chrome-legged table. What we had was old stuff other farmwomen had hidden away in their barns and attics. But thanks to my hard work and the Spic'n Span, what we had sparkled.

I poured the man a cup of Butternut coffee and dished up a wedge of the cherry pie I'd baked for the Happy Homemaker's 4-H club meeting I was hostessing that night. I'd have to hustle to roll out another crust, but the sacrifice seemed worth it. My dad had died of polio when I was three, and finding Mom a new husband had become a hobby of mine. I wasn't above stretching the elastic on the truth if I thought it would help.

"Here, you have to try a piece of Mom's cherry pie. She makes the flakiest crusts in the county," I said, sitting down across the table from him.

Between bites, he asked, "Might you know

how long it's been since water flowed in the dry creek bed to the south?"

"Mom says there hasn't been any real water there since she was a girl. She says it was fed by a spring and that the spring dried up during the droughts they had back then, though sometimes, when we've had a lot of rain, there are puddles."

"Great pie," he said, saluting with his fork. "And the pasture, the one in the southeast corner of your section, how many people would you guess turn off the main highway and drive by there on a given day?"

"Hardly anyone. There aren't any houses on that mile, so no one needs to use it every day, and most everyone who lives around here uses one of the other roads because they're safer. The train crossing on the road you're asking about is sort of hidden by a sharp curve on one side and a bridge on the other."

"Thanks, you've been very helpful," he said, sliding his chair back as if he were about to leave.

"More coffee?" I asked just as Mom walked in, dressed in her bib overalls.

"This man's here to see you, Mom. I invited him in and gave him a slice of *your* pie."

"Whatever it is you're selling, we can't afford to buy it." Mom used that line with every sales-man who came around. We were, and still are, land rich and cash poor. Our farm is worth a lot of money, if we sold it. Mom would never do that, so we live on the "cash poor" half of the farm economics equation.

"Guess I should introduce myself. Name's Bob Carter and I'm with the federal government." He smiled through perfect rows of Pepsodent teeth.

"Department of Agriculture?"

"No, ma'am. I'm with the Department of Defense." He pulled his wallet out of his vest pocket and flashed an official-looking ID card. "We're planning to lease your sister's pasture land for an air force project, and she said you might be able to answer some questions."

Mom's brow puckered. The pasture he was talking about was our meadow. Except for the coldest winter months and planting or harvest time, Mom and I spent our Sunday afternoons in the meadow. We'd spread a quilt across the grass, and Mom would tell me stories about the way things used to be, stories about my dad and about the two pioneer women who were buried there. The meadow was the place where Mom had taught me all the important things. About the birds and the bees, both the real ones and the other kind. About what it takes to be a friend to people, to animals, to the land. The meadow was like an Easter dress, a thing that was beautiful and made you feel special.

It was true, the meadow belonged to my aunt

Jane. My grandparents had willed it to her, but she never went there, so it had been easy to pretend it belonged to us.

"What kind of project?" Mom asked.

"Can't say. But I can tell you this: when we're finished you and your daughter will feel a whole lot safer."

"Feel perfectly safe now, and until you can tell me what you plan to do there, I'm not answering any questions."

"There's no need to get defensive, ma'am. That pasture's worthless as it stands now. Fallow land, never been put into production."

"Not fallow. *Spared* land. One of the few patches of virgin prairie left in the county, and my parents' will stipulated that it was never to be plowed. Did my sister happen to mention that?" Mom's voice was like a pressure cooker building up too much steam.

"We've studied the deed, ma'am, so we are well aware of the no-plow clause."

"But you're planning to spoil it one way or another, right?"

"Can't say, but that will be our right once the lease is signed. Like I said, when we're finished you'll thank us."

The pressure cooker blew. "I'll be thanking you now. Thanking you to leave."

"Okay, I'll go. Your daughter already answered the questions I came out here to ask." He turned to me then. "Could you hold back that dog so I can get to my car?"

I didn't have to look at Mom to know she'd want me to do as Mr. Carter had asked.

When I returned to the kitchen, Mom was already dialing the phone. "Is Jane there?" she asked. "You know darn well who this is, Buck. Now please put Jane on the phone."

While Mom waited for Aunt Jane to come on the line, she cupped her hand over the mouthpiece. "What questions did that Mr. Carter ask?"

I looked at the floor. "I'm sorry. I didn't know."

"I'm not angry with you. I just need to know what you told him so I can begin to make sense of what's going on."

"He asked me when was the last time water flowed in the creek."

"Good lord, they're worried about water levels, which means they're planning to dig." She pulled her hand away from the phone and said, "Jane, we need to talk."

Although Mom had offered to drive into town, Jane insisted that she would come to the farm instead, and as usual, she took her time, not arriving until late afternoon. Also as usual, Jane was wearing the same poorly sewn red dress she always wore when she came to our house, the same crimson lipstick, the same beehive hairdo, and the same spiked heels, which left dents in the kitchen linoleum.

As soon as Aunt Jane sat down at the kitchen table, she fished a pack of Marlboros from her see-through plastic purse and lit up. Mom frowned but didn't say anything to Jane. Instead she asked me to find something Jane could use for an ashtray. By the time I got back to the table with a chipped saucer, Jane had already flicked ash on the floor I'd scrubbed and waxed earlier that morning.

"What's this I hear about the meadow?" Mom asked in a voice that was almost friendly.

"It's mine. I can do whatever I like with it."

"That's true, it is yours, but I hope you haven't forgotten that Mama wanted the meadow to stay the way it's always been."

"Mama was a fool," Jane said, grinding out her cigarette in the saucer.

Mom rubbed her forehead as if she had a headache coming on, then she leaned forward and said, "If it's the money you need, why don't you lease the meadow to me? What have they offered to pay you, twenty-five or thirty dollars a month?"

Jane grinned. "You're not even close. They're going to pay me two thousand dollars a year, and they've promised Buck a ten-dollar-an-hour job."

Mom fell back in her chair as if someone had shoved her. "Those are bankers' wages. What kind of work have they asked him to do?"

"Night security. Once construction begins, he'll be in charge of keeping trespassers out."

"Construction?" Mom and I blurted in unison.

"What are they planning to do?" Mom asked.

"It's all very hush-hush."

"We're family," Mom said. "You know the secret will be safe with me."

"Right. The way you kept Mama and Daddy's will a secret from me."

"I couldn't tell you what I didn't know."

Jane took her time lighting another cigarette; then, her words tangled with smoke, she said, "Oh, you knew all right, knew all the way to the bank. Now it's my turn."

Mom rubbed her forehead again. "Is there anything I can do to change your mind?"

"Sure, you can give me back what's rightfully mine, half of this farm."

"So Buck can bankrupt this farm just like he did with his own?" Mom said under her breath.

Jane stubbed out her cigarette. "That's the deal, take it or leave it."

Mom just shook her head.

"Fine," Jane said getting up. "It wouldn't make any difference anyway. Bob Carter says the government's got the right to take the meadow whether I sign or not, says they've got the right to eminent domain, whatever that is."

At the door, Jane turned and said, "You ladies have a nice day." Then she was gone.

I swished my hand back and forth, trying to clear the smoky air, then said, "Jane doesn't know about the women buried in the meadow, does she?"

"No. You and Mama are the only ones I've ever told. I guess I figured my secret was safe as long as the meadow wasn't plowed."

"What is eminent domain, anyway?"

"I think I know, but why don't we look in the dictionary to make sure I've got it right."

It took me only a minute to run into the parlor, take the dictionary down from the shelf, and return to the kitchen, where I speed-flipped to the right page. "'The power of government to take private property for public use, with just compensation.' That's not fair," I said.

"Doesn't seem so, does it? They can waltz in, spoil the meadow seven ways to Sunday, as long as they pay. They could drain the entire Department of Defense budget, and there still wouldn't be enough money to pay what the meadow's worth. It'd be like trying to hang a price tag on a star."

"Whatever they want to do, we're going to stop them, right?"

"We sure are going to try, and I think we'd best start by calling Bert Black, see if he can give us some legal advice."

Mom called Bert right away. I knew from her face that the news wasn't good. Later she told me that he'd said he'd look into it and get back to her, but that he believed winning a case against the government was about as likely as landing a man on the moon.

The 4-H meeting went on as scheduled that night, though I bungled my bound buttonhole demonstration badly.

Early the next morning, Mom kept the long-distance operator busy, placing calls to our congressmen in Washington, D.C. They weren't in, but Mom left messages with their aides. One did call back, and he promised Mom he'd look into it. That was the last we heard from him.

If you had been looking into a window on our lives that week, you might have thought nothing had changed. Mom baled the field of alfalfa she had mowed and raked the week before, butchered a hog, and helped one of the ewes birth twin lambs. I retrieved warm eggs from beneath the breasts of the setting hens, unpegged billowing sheets from the clothesline, and uprooted wiry weeds from the vegetable garden. But if that window had opened on our minds, you would have seen the spin and heard the whir, like the workings behind the face of the old grandfather clock. That one perfect idea, like a four-leafed gem of clover — that's what our minds were searching for. It wasn't until Sunday afternoon in the meadow that we found it.

The bees were bad. They descended on us soon after I had tipped the Thermos and filled our glasses with cherry Kool-Aid. There were dozens of them buzzing their little wings, then boldly landing on the rim of the glass. When one tried to follow a sip into my mouth, I turned to Mom and said, "I give up. The bees win. Let's go back to the house."

Mom's face lit up, bright, as if she'd seen God. "Repeat what you just said."

"I give up, the bees win?"

"Sarah, you've done it. You've found our one perfect answer. If all else fails, we'll become like the bees — drive the government away with our peskiness. Let's go back to the house and make ourselves a nice long list."

We laughed that day, for the first time since Bob Carter had come to call. Laughed at the thought of our zaniest ideas, laughed as we imagined the most brilliant ones. Laughed until our sides ached, laughed ourselves into a honey of a plan.

The only problem was that we didn't know when the construction would begin. Without her knowing it, Aunt Jane helped us out. She got in the habit of phoning to give what Mom called "salt in the wound" progress reports. Jane had signed the papers. She'd gotten her first lease check. Buck would begin work on Monday night next.

When Mom put the receiver down after that last call, she turned to me and said, "There's one more phrase I want you to look up in the dictionary before we call out the bees."

I did, and listed directly below "civil defense," I found the definition for "civil disobedience." "'Refusal to obey civil laws in an effort to induce change in governmental policy or legislation, characterized by the use of passive resistance or other nonviolent means.'"

"It's your choice," Mom said when I closed the dictionary. "I don't want to involve you in something that you're not comfortable with."

I thought about it for exactly one heartbeat, then flapped my elbows and hummed buzzing bee noises through my teeth.

We saw the mushrooming gravel cloud before we saw the navy blue air force truck. It pulled off to the side of the road that bordered the southeast corner of the meadow. Two men loaded down with surveying gear got out. I ducked under the branches of a weeping willow where Mom was waiting, and we watched as they began wading through the grass. One man walked a few paces ahead of the other, as if he was in charge, and it was his yelp we heard when his shin came into contact with the half-hidden electric fencing wire. Ordinarily I would have felt sorry for him, forgiven him for the foul words that sparked off his tongue, but this was war, a holy war of sorts. I gave Mom the thumbs up.

When both men had hurdled the wire, Mom let go of Ferdinand's halter and slapped him hard on his rump. He took off, hoofs throwing up divots of meadow earth. You would have thought those men had seen a real-life Purple People Eater, the way they dropped their equipment and hightailed it back to their truck. Ferdinand, who Mom had said was smarter than your average bull, stopped short of the wire. He snorted. He pawed. He paced.

After the men drove away, Mom called Ferdinand in. She had a way with animals, especially the ones she had raised. Though I had to keep my distance, with Mom Ferdinand was as gentle as a newborn calf.

When the men returned later that afternoon, the one who had been shocked by the electric wire was toting a rifle. Mom had guessed as much. By then Ferdinand was munching oats in his stall in the barn. Time had come for the bees, the real ones. Mom had had something besides cross-pollination in mind when she'd drizzled squiggly threads of sorghum molasses in circles around the abandoned surveying equipment, being extra careful not to damage the instruments themselves. The men began swatting the air before they got within ten feet.

The bees drove the men away. But like a bad case of the hiccups, they returned armed with weapons to fight the last problem they had run up against. The netted beekeepers' hats didn't do them much good when faced with the dead forty-foot tree trunk Mom had hitched behind the tractor and dragged across the road. Not much good at all.

By late Thursday afternoon, all they had managed to accomplish was to plant a dozen or so small red surveying flags, which Mom and I were having so much fun rearranging we didn't hear Uncle Buck sneak up behind us. "Caught you two red-handed," he said, a strong smell of beer on his breath.

"Just picking up some trash that blew in," Mom said, straightening her back.

"I know what you are trying to do, Anna, but it isn't going to work."

"What is it you think I'm doing?"

"Trespassing, for a start, and engaging in subversive acts against the United States government. Why, as far as I know, you might even be one of those communist sympathizers."

"She is not. She is not a communist," I said.

"Aren't you a feisty one." He reached out and ran his hand slowly down my arm. I shrugged away.

"Don't you ever lay a hand on Sarah again," Mom said, stepping in front of me. "Not ever."

"Damn it all, Anna, I've got a job to do here. If they figure out it's my sister-in-law that's behind all the delays, they'll can me. If you try any of your funny business tomorrow morning when the heavy equipment arrives, I'll call the sheriff, and he'll haul your uppity butt off to jail."

"What now?" I asked as we watched Buck walk back to his truck.

"Sarah, until now what we've done has been fairly harmless, but the thing I have to do tomorrow, I have to do alone."

"No, Mom. We're in this together. You said so yourself. You said this meadow belongs to me, too."

"It does belong to you. But I can't risk any harm coming to you at the hands of men like Buck. Tomorrow, when they come, you won't be anywhere within shouting distance."

"But — "

"No buts about it," she said in a tone that I had learned meant she'd buried the subject.

"What do you plan to do? Will you at least let me share in that?"

"I will tell you later tonight. I want to do something I haven't done for years. I want to spend the night here in the meadow."

"What about Buck?"

"If tonight's like every other night since he's been on guard, he'll be asleep in his truck by the time the sun goes down."

Mom had been right about Buck. That night, when we sneaked up on his truck, careful not to kick the beer cans that littered the ground, Buck was snoring.

A safe distance away, we settled ourselves on the friendship quilt my grandmother Rebecca's Quilting Guild had once made.

"Tell me what it is you plan to do tomorrow."

"In the morning, when they come, I'm going to lay myself down in the grass, right over the spot where I buried Abigail, and I'm not going to budge, at least not on my own. I've called Sam Flynn at the newspaper, told him that if he comes out here nice and early, I'll have a story for him. I'm thinking, maybe if this whole thing is as hush-hush as Jane says it is, the air force people won't want any publicity, and they'll find some other piece of land for their dirty work."

"Do you think that will stop them?"

"Maybe, maybe not. But I can't just let them come in here and spoil this land while I stand back and do nothing, and this is the only thing I know to do."

"Do you think Buck will call the sheriff?"

"I suppose he will. And listen carefully now. If the sheriff does put me in jail, you'll need to call Bert Black and ask him to find out how much bail money it will take to get me out. Then call Roy Paulson. He's been hounding me to sell him Ferdinand. He's a good man. He'll give you a fair price. If it's still not enough, call Maud MaCoy and ask her to drive you into town. Take that old gold coin and my wedding ring to Rockcastle Jewelers and have them appraised. And call old Joe Knott. He's retired and living in town now, but if you ask him real sweet, he'll come out to help you with the chores. Can you do that for me, keep things running until I get back? We Foster women can do anything, can't we?"

"Anything."

Mom reached for my right hand. "It's time for me to pass this along." She slipped a thin gold ring on my finger — Abigail's ring, the woman Mom had buried in the meadow, the woman who had loved the meadow first.

In the distance, a coyote howled. Fireflies

blinked on and off. A breeze rustled in the grass. The black velvet sky shimmered with star sequins. I wanted to reach up, pull the sky down, and hold it against my cheek.

I must have fallen asleep sometime during the night because I awoke to a rumble.

"They're here," Mom whispered.

I tried to rub the fog from my eyes, but it didn't rub off because the fog was real, hanging like a wet blanket in the air.

"It's time. Get on up to the house and bolt the door. If I'm not back by noon, start making those calls."

Numb from sleep and new worry over the thing Mom was about to do, I walked in a path that would lead me straight to the house. When I neared the trees, I steered right, toward the weeping willow. I crouched there, straining to see through the mist. Men's voices shouted over the clank of gears and the roar of engines.

After a time, a breeze picked up, thinning the fog into a gauzy haze and revealing two lopsided wooden crosses that peeked above the meadow grass. "Hold up," a voice shouted. The engine noise shifted into a purring idle. Two figures approached the crosses. One was Buck, and the other was Gus Goodman, the sheriff. I looked for Mr. Flynn from the newspaper, hoping he was lagging a few paces behind. He wasn't.

"Anna, you and I have known each other for years. If you leave now, there won't be any trouble," said Sheriff Goodman.

This was followed by a long silence.

"Anna, you know I don't want to do this."

More silence.

"You give me no choice then. Anna Foster, you are under arrest for trespassing on government property and for — "

Buck stepped forward then and finished the sheriff's sentence. "For subversive acts that have kept those nice fellows over there from getting down to the work of erecting an Atlas missile launch silo in this worthless piece of pasture."

There was no air-raid siren, no time to duck for cover before the flash of brilliant white light. "No. Not here, not in our meadow, not anywhere," I shrieked as I raced toward them. "Not here. Not here." My fists pounded on Buck's chest. "Not anywhere."

Buck grabbed my wrists.

"Not — " Mom's fist whizzed past my ear and landed with a thud on Buck's jaw. His knees buckled, and his hands went limp just before he slumped to the ground.

"You okay?" Mom asked, her eyes in a panic.

"No, Mom. Did you hear what Buck said?"

Sheriff Goodman helped Buck up. Buck spat blood from his mouth, then said, "Add two counts of assault on a government employee to your list of charges, Gus."

"Don't be telling me what I should and shouldn't do," the sheriff said to Buck before turning to Mom. "I think we'd better go into town, talk things through before this gets out of hand."

"You want me to cuff them?" Buck asked.

"If there's any cuffing, it'll be me doing it."

"There's no need for handcuffs. I'll come along with you, make no fuss, if you leave Sarah out of this."

"I think she'll be safer with me," he said, shooting a glance at Buck.

"Maybe you're right. But there is one thing I need you to promise me before we go. There are two women buried here, the first right under this spot, where we stand. The other under that cross over yonder."

"Nice try, Anna," Buck said.

"It's true. One was buried here during pioneer times. The other I buried myself, back in 1936."

"You probably badmouthed her to death," Buck said, rubbing his jaw.

"Gus, you'll see to it then? See that their remains stay undisturbed until I've had time to make arrangements at the cemetery in town?"

"I'll talk to the head engineer. He seems like a reasonable man, and I'd guess those hard-hat fellows who run the heavy equipment wouldn't be too keen on the idea of digging up bones. Why don't you and your daughter wait in my car."

From the back seat of the sheriff's car, with my nose pressed to the window, I watched as wide swatches of prairie grass and wildflowers were crushed under the spiked tracks of an army of Caterpillars and backhoes. Frightened jack rabbits ducked for cover down tunnels to their underground homes. Sparrows, larks, and mourning doves rose in great clouds from the trees. A monarch butterfly landed on the window. I rolled down the window, hoping she would fly in. She didn't. She fluttered straight for the center of the meadow, where, like a prehistoric beast come back to life, a backhoe's steel jaws ripped a hole in the earth. Its monstrous head reared and swung right, dribbling dirt from its rusty chin.

Sheriff Goodman drove us home, and no charges were ever filed. He did ask Mom to promise that she'd steer clear of the construction site. Mom didn't actually promise. She just said, "What good would it do? The damage has already been done."

We steered clear only until dusk, when we made our way to the weeping willow. The meadow floor, except for a roped-off square around the two crosses, had been stripped naked. We didn't stay long.

More than three years have passed, and the missile has crouched deep in the earth, waiting, for half that time. We don't know what kind of nuclear device it harbors in its nose cone. I imagine whatever type it is, if it accidentally went off, it would be flash, *pouf* — history for all of Prairie County. And that says nothing of the Soviet missile that probably has our rural route address programmed into its guidance system. The silo is restricted, but it's no secret.

A twelve-foot chainlink fence, rimmed with an outward jut of barbed wire, stands guard around the silo's borders. Floodlights, perched on the tops of tall, creosoted poles, erase the stars with their brilliant white light. There is an angled, concrete structure that rises above the ground. We think these are stairs to some underground control room because we've seen young airmen, with only two or three stripes on their sleeves, go in and come out.

In the center of it all is a circle of concrete, about fifty feet in diameter. Within this circle, strips of steel trace the outline of the silo doors. Beneath the doors is the missile.

I've seen it — once when it was lowered in and

again on October 16 of last year, the night JFK had set as the deadline for the Soviets to turn their ships away from Cuban shores.

Mom had been harvesting corn that day, and when she came in for supper, she told me that a steady stream of military vehicles had been raising dust clouds on the gravel road. I left the dirty dishes in the sink, a thing I never did, and we headed for the weeping willow. We'd been there only a short time when the silo doors opened to a perpendicular position. The missile slowly rose until its full sixty-five-foot height was exposed. About halfway up the side of its silvery skin was a symbol — a man's steel fist grasping a lightning bolt.

I don't know if they actually tested the propulsion system that night, because we didn't stick around long enough to find out. After I'd rounded up Brutus and as many cats as I could find, I went into the cave. Mom joined me there, not because she believed being underground would save us, but because I'd asked her to. As I sat there, I imagined other missiles rising out of other silos, out of other meadows and fields, all across the prairie states — Nebraska, the Dakotas, Kansas, Wyoming — and wondered if there were other girls, other mothers, huddled in caves. Caves whose air was dank and hard to breathe. Caves whose walls seemed to shrink with each explosive tick of the wind-up clock. Shrink until close, like the walls of a coffin. Closer, like a crushing new layer of skin. Squeezing in, until there was nearly nothing left of me.

I shot out of the cave like a missile being launched. I gulped in air, gulped and gulped, then turned to Mom and said, "I'm never going down in the cave again. Never." And I haven't, not even when we've had bad storms. And I won't. Sticking my head in the sand like an ostrich didn't solve anything. President Kennedy had said, "Ask not what your country can do for you. Ask what you can do for your country." And that is what I intend to do.

So, dear future daughter, this is my story. I hope there is more, hope that by the time you are born the threat of nuclear war is a topic found only in history books. Be patient. In one way or another I will help make it so.

Nine

The last pages in Sarah's notebook displayed pressed flowers, each covered with a square of plastic wrap, which was taped to the paper on all four sides. Beneath each flower was a handwritten name. Prairie wild rose. Chicory. Dame's rocket. Queen Anne's lace. Queen Anne's lace! I moved the notebook closer to the candle. The stem was there, but time had crumbled the flower's white petals into a sad, ashy memory of itself. It hurt my eyes to look at it, so I turned to the last page. Taped there was an enlarged color photo of the field where I had scattered my mother's ashes. No. That wasn't possible. Or was it? There *were* trees in the background, like the trees that had grown along the small creek. And mixed in with the green, were splashes of white. Queen Anne's lace? I lifted the candle, held it as close as I dared, and squinted, but couldn't make out the snowflake pattern in the blur. There was only one way to know for sure.

The veranda roof was steeper than the roof

over the back porch and slippery with rain-soaked moss. Using my flashlight, I found the place where the rose trellis was attached to the roof and lowered one foot over the edge, testing the first rung for strength. It felt solid, so I started down. One rung, then a second. Snap, and the rest was all fall. A thud. One last loud snap and pain exploded in my left arm.

I knew my arm was broken. I knew because it was the same sound I'd heard, the same kind of pain I'd felt, when the drunk driver had broadsided our car. A paramedic had put my arm in a sling, but not before prying me away from my mother, her eyes still blinking, her chest still moving up and down. "Where will I find you?" I'd screamed as he'd carried me through a swirl of red ambulance lights.

"In the meadow," I now said, picking myself up. "I believe I will find you in the meadow." I shifted my backpack to the front and slid my left wrist under one of the shoulder straps. I *was* going to the meadow, and a broken arm wasn't going to stop me. Though I'd never been there myself, I owned a map. A map drawn not with pencil and paper but with words — Abby's words, Rebecca's words, Anna's, Sarah's.

Navigating the cottonwood grove was hard. Many fallen trees lay in my path. I climbed over some, walked around others, each step jostling my arm, causing it to throb.

The maze ended at the creek, which I heard before I reached it. There was water in it, churned up and running fast. I had to get across, would get across, but how? Wading wasn't an option because of my arm, but more important, because of my backpack. I couldn't risk getting it and its contents wet. Instead of going back the way I'd come, I decided I'd get to the meadow faster if I worked my way along the creek until I found the road bridge Sarah had mentioned.

This was harder than I'd thought. Mud sucked at my shoes, and low-growing tree branches slapped me in the face. Each duck or weave, each slip of my foot, caused pain to shoot up my arm.

I hadn't gotten very far when I came upon a dead tree blocking my path. I shone my flashlight along its length. It lay from one bank of the creek to the other. Its diameter was the size of a hug. I quickly kicked off my shoes and, using only my right hand, knotted a lace from each shoe to belt loops on my shorts.

With one foot in front of the other, and balancing with one arm, I started across. The rushing creek water sprayed cold droplets at my toes and the craggy bark. My muddy shoes flopped against my thighs. Halfway across, I teetered. Left. Right. Left. Then, imagining for myself a pair of sturdy wings, I found my balance and continued until I was safely on the other side.

I rested for a moment, but only a moment, then

put my shoes back on and made my way through the cottonwood maze on the far side of the creek and into the meadow. I walked a few steps into the knee-high grass, then stopped and drew in a deep breath. The air was heavy with a familiar scent — earthy yet sweet. I drew in an even deeper breath. And with that second breath, my body remembered. It was the scent of the field, the field I had searched for and never found, the field of my dream. My hand trembled as I aimed the flashlight straight down. A puddle of light circled my feet, just as it always had in the dream. "Where will I find you?" I shouted. I listened for an answer — listened with my ears, listened with my soul — but there was no answer.

I shone my flashlight across the meadow. What I hoped to find I don't know. A place to rest, maybe. A place to still the ache. What I found, at the far edge of the flashlight's reach, was the concrete stairwell Sarah had described in her story. I started toward it.

The stairwell's top was flat, but a few feet back it slanted at right angles toward the ground. The taller end housed a rust-pocked door, frozen in a position just wide enough for me to squeeze through. Inside, I shone my light down a steep tunnel of steps. If I hadn't been hurting, I might have gone down those steps, explored whatever was down there. But I *was* hurting, so I sat on the landing and carefully slid my throbbing arm out of the backpack strap. I laid the flashlight, which was growing dim, on the floor in front of me, then lifted the baggie out of the backpack and did something I'd never done before. With the tip of the baggie gripped between my teeth, I opened both the outer and inner Ziplocs with my good hand, then balanced the baggie in the hollow of my crossed legs. I licked a finger and pressed it into the ashes. A thin layer of ashes stuck. I rubbed the ashes over my swollen arm. I waited. The hurt didn't go away.

Fighting back tears, I felt around inside my backpack until I found the small sketchpad and a pencil. I pulled these out, then licked all the fingers of my drawing hand and pressed them, one at a time, into the baggie. If my mother wasn't in the meadow, I would draw her there. I had just begun the sketch when the flashlight's battery died. But I didn't stop drawing. When the sketch was finished, I leaned my back into the cool concrete wall. Waited.

I heard something then, a far away voice or a close-up whisper, I wasn't sure which. I listened. Nothing at first, then I heard the voice again, far away, but nearer than before.

"Hope, are you here?"

"I'm here, Mother," I cried, leaping to my feet and squeezing through the door.

A light flickered in the distance. I looked down, expecting my feet to be locked in a puddle of light, like before. No light bound my feet. I was free. I ran, but only a few steps. My arm hurt, bad. That's when I knew I wasn't in the dream, that the voice wasn't my mother's voice, that the person hurrying toward me, the person holding the lantern, was Sarah.

"Oh, Hope. I'm so glad I've found you," Sarah shouted, waving her hand over her head.

When she reached me, she set her lantern down, and then hugged me. A lightning bolt of pain shot up my arm. I stiffened and pulled away, turning my head so Sarah wouldn't see that I was crying.

"What is it, Hope? Are you upset because I was gone so long?"

I shook my head.

"Tell me what it is then. Maybe I can help."

How could I tell her that I was crying because I'd wanted the person carrying the light, the person running toward me, to be my mother? How could I say a hurtful thing like that?

"I've broken my arm," I said instead.

Sarah reached for the lantern. "Let me have a look."

Sarah gasped. "Sit down here on the silo and I'll make a sling," she said, unbuttoning the top button of her shirt.

Anna arrived just then. "You okay? When I

saw the shattered rose trellis I was afraid you'd broken a leg."

"An arm," Sarah said, taking off her shirt.

"Darned trellis. I should have torn that thing down years ago, when it first began to rot. Sarah, do you want me to go back to the house and bring your car around?"

Sarah had just finished tying the shirt sling around my neck. "That'd be great, Mom. And while you're at it, bring me a shirt. The people at the hospital might get the wrong idea if I show up wearing only a bra."

"Better you than me," Anna chuckled, then said, "I think I'll go by way of the road this time. I almost earned my wings tightrope walking on the trunk of a cottonwood that has fallen across the creek."

"You didn't!" Sarah said.

"Had to. There hasn't been this much water in the creek since I was a girl. I followed your footprints, Hope, saw that they ended at the tree. I figured if you were brave enough to cross, I'd give it a try. Now I'm off. Be back in a jiff."

I felt around on the concrete for my backpack, then remembered I'd left it in the stairwell. I started to stand up, but a wave of dizziness made me sit down.

I then asked Sarah a question I'd rarely asked anyone. "Could you do me a favor?"

"Name it, and it's as good as done."

"I left my backpack in the stairwell. Could you get it for me?"

"I'd love to."

Part of Sarah walked away, but another part stayed with me in the scent of her shirt, a mixture of baby lotion and the not unpleasant scent of work. And something else I couldn't name. Worry, maybe.

When Sarah returned, she laid the backpack in my lap. "It was pitch-black in there, but I groped around until I found it. It amazes me that you can carry that kind of weight on your shoulders. It must weigh ten pounds."

It weighed more than that. I knew this because I'd once weighed it on a bathroom scale, and it had gotten even heavier since then.

"This isn't the way I'd hoped to introduce you to our meadow. I'd wanted you to see it first in daylight."

"I feel like I have," I said. "I saw the photograph in your notebook."

"You read my story then? I'm glad. Do you have any questions?"

Searching for a safe question, I asked, "I was wondering what happened to the graves?"

"Actually, nothing. You can't see them in the dark, but they are marked by wooden crosses, which Mom replaces every few years."

"Does the meadow belong to Anna now?"

"Yes and no. It's still Jane's land, but Mom

leases it from her, pays her the same two thousand dollars a year the air force paid before they abandoned this site in 1968. They removed the missile, but little else. You've probably guessed that we are sitting on top of the missile silo right now."

I shifted, the concrete seeming harder than before.

"Mom and I have been restoring the meadow ever since. We dismantled the chainlink fence and the guardhouse, erased the service road, reintroduced the bluestem grass, the wildflowers. It's taken us nearly thirty summers to do the work we've done. When you've had a chance to see it in the light, you will see for yourself how lovely it is today. But I'm afraid no amount of nurturing will restore the meadow to the way she was before. Just when we think she has finally healed herself, a rash of musk thistle sprouts, seemingly overnight."

"Maybe the meadow can't forget."

"I suppose you're right. I need to be more patient, give her whatever time she needs. But I won't give up on her." Sarah held out her hand then. "Feel that, it's started raining again."

I looked up, but it wasn't the rain that gave me a sudden chill. Headlights sliced two white paths across the grass. Headlights in the dark, blurred by rain. There was something remembered in their glare. Eight years evaporated, and I was six again, sitting next to my mother.

I thrust my hand into the backpack, desperate to touch her. She wasn't there.

I don't remember the car stopping or Anna getting out. All I remember is running toward the stairwell. Sarah caught up to me as I was about to slide through the door.

Stepping in front of me, she said, "We need to go."

"I've lost something, and I can't leave until I've found it."

"Whatever it is you've lost, it can't be as important as having a doctor look at that arm."

"It is more important. More important than anything."

"Tell me what it is, and we'll look for it together."

"A Ziploc baggie," I whispered.

"Where did you last have it?"

I pointed toward the door.

"I don't think it's in there, Hope, or I would have found it when I found the backpack."

"It has to be," I said, pushing past her.

Sarah followed me in with her lantern, but the only things there were the small sketchpad, pencil, and flashlight. *Think,* I said to myself. I'd taken the baggie out of the backpack, opened it, and laid it in my lap. Had it still been there when I'd heard the voice calling me? When I'd leapt up? Had it caught on my clothes or clung to my muddy shoes?

I burst outside, my eyes frantically searching, my arms flailing at the rain-soaked grass.

Later Sarah would tell me that both she and Anna tried to talk to me, tried to stop me from swinging my broken arm. But I remember no voices, no pain. I was focused on only one thing — finding my mother.

I found the baggie, gaping, wet, and empty, in the grass about halfway between the stairwell and the circular silo slab. I dropped to my knees, thinking I might be able to scoop some of the ashes up. But there was nothing to save. The rain had washed her away.

Sarah knelt beside me. "What was in the baggie, Hope? What is it that you've lost?"

"My mother. I . . . I've lost my mother's ashes," I answered, dissolving into tears.

In the emergency room at the Prairie Hill Hospital, while we were waiting for the results of my x-rays, Anna reached into her pocket and pulled out my sketchpad. "I almost forgot this. You dropped it back in the meadow. This picture you drew is a perfect likeness of Sarah."

I looked at the sketch, looked at Sarah, then

back at the sketch, the one I'd drawn while blind-
ed by the dark. I had no explanation, but instead
of sketching my mother's face, I'd sketched
Sarah's.

"May I see?" Sarah said, leaning forward. "Yes,
it does look like me. The mouth, the nose, the
eyes." Her face lit up like a Christmas tree.

Ten

A year has passed since that night in the meadow. Sarah and I did return to Minneapolis, but only long enough for her to resign her position at the university and to arrange for my adoption. All those years, I'd thought adoption meant cheating my mother's memory. I was wrong. The person I was cheating was me. It took losing my mother a second time for me to see that.

Sarah and I are working hard at becoming a mother and a daughter. It hasn't always been easy, but we've come a long way. I've told her about my years in foster care, about my years of searching, about the accident, and about the dream.

Sarah teaches part time at the local community college. Anna is teaching, too, teaching Sarah how to farm. All fall and winter Sarah pored over books and articles on earth-friendly agricultural practices. Then, this spring, using Anna's old-time machinery, she planted corn on the same plot of land Abby's father had broken open and, in another field, a crop of happy sunflowers. I even planted a few not-so-straight rows myself.

The barn isn't sad anymore because animals, my animals, are living there now. Anna is teaching me animal husbandry. In August I will show Straw at the county fair. She's still a bit stubborn on the lead, but we're working on that. She's also much larger than most Holstein yearlings, probably because of all the milk I bucket-fed her after Eb Pinkney gave her to me.

I have lambs, Queen and Lace, and too many chickens to name. And I have Choice, my dog. I named her Choice because, of all the dogs at the animal shelter, she was the one I *chose* to adopt. Though Choice is free to wander anywhere on the farm a sniff leads her, she doesn't sleep in the barn. She sleeps with me.

Anna is still Anna, always there when I need her, always knowing just the right thing to say. This winter she hatched a brilliant idea for a project the three of us could work on together — a story quilt. On large squares of white fabric, we appliquéd bits of cloth we'd cut from old clothing that had been stored in trunks up in the attic. Abby's square has a sod house, and Rebecca's, a blue dress. On her square, Anna embroidered a circle of words — "To Everything There Is a Season." Shimmering inside this circle are a dozen gold coins. Before she began work on her square, Sarah asked if we thought a mushroom cloud would be a bit much.

"A bit," Anna answered.

"How about my lattice-topped cherry pie?"

"Go for it," I said, and she did. Her square looks good enough to eat.

I had no trouble deciding the thing my square would represent. I even provided the fabric — a carefully cut circle of red nylon surrounding Garfield's mended smile.

There are other squares on the quilt. Among these are butterflies and bumblebees; a silver thimble, a gold ring, and a rainbow of polished stones; a painter's palette and a shovel; a barn, chicken coop, and house, complete with a mended rose trellis. In the center of the squares is the meadow, which is pieced together from tiny squares of solid greens and riotous florals and is laid out in a way that tricks the eye into believing it is a watercolor painting.

Anna presented the finished quilt to me, as a gift for my fifteenth birthday. Sleep happens easier now. My birthday gift from Sarah — Abby's gold ring.

Sarah's old bedroom, my bedroom, has undergone a change, too. The old posters are gone. Well, not really gone. They are stored in the attic. In their place hang my favorite sketches. My memories and old earth-finds now occupy the dresser tops and shelves.

I add new memories regularly. The latest is a corsage that Lloyd Stuhr's son, Jake, gave me when he escorted me to Prairie Hill High's freshman dance. Jake's cool. He didn't even flinch when he came to the door and saw that I was wearing this funky dress Anna had worn to her high school graduation. Last week I took Jake for a joy ride on the Cushman. We didn't mind one bit when she ran out of gas.

Now that school is out, I spend a lot of time in the meadow, often working beside Sarah and Anna. The meadow is fragile. You can still see the ruts that the tires on Sarah's car made the night I broke my arm. But the meadow is tough, too. Anna says she's sprouting fewer weeds than ever before.

One day I asked Sarah if the silo could be removed. "We talked about that, in the beginning, but I couldn't bear the thought of having bulldozers rip the meadow apart again."

Anna, who was pulling weeds nearby, added, "I like to think of it as the meadow's badge of courage."

It's a badge I've been embellishing. I've recently finished painting a mural on the outside of the stairwell. In the background, using shades of greens and yellows, I've tried to mimic the sway and rhythm of the bluestem grass. To this, I've added the idea of wildflowers. A splash of red here, a spatter of blue there, whites, pinks, and lavenders. In the foreground, I've painted larger-than-life faces — Abby and Rebecca on one of the upright walls, Anna and Sarah on the other. I was going to stop there, but Sarah insisted that I belonged in the mural, too. I'd never tried to draw my face before, so when it was time to make the practice sketch, I sat at the mirrored vanity table. I'd look, then draw; look, then draw. When the sketch was finished, I held it next to my face so I could see both my sketched face and my real face side by side in the mirror. What I saw took my breath away. The thing I'd longed for, the thing I'd tried for so many years to capture, had been there all along. My mother's face — reflected in my own. My face, our face, now looks skyward from the surface of the slanted wall.

The future? I'll keep drawing, that much I know. And painting. I've recently been eyeing the broad, windowless side of Anna's barn. College? Sarah says the University of Nebraska has an outstanding art department. But that's three years away, and I'm no longer in a hurry to reach the age of eighteen. Now I can live my life one day at a time, knowing I'll still be here tomorrow. I'm part of a family now, a family not bound by time. Abby is here, in the sway of the cedar trees. Rebecca, too, in the magical, lifting light of the meadow. Anna, dear Anna, the keeper of the stories, the keeper of this land. And Sarah, my mom.

I haven't forgotten my first mother. I think of her often, especially when I'm in the meadow, where I am just now. She's here, in this handful of rich, black soil, in this shimmering drop of dew, and here, in the fragrant petals of this wild prairie rose. She's here, alongside the others, holding up the earth.